THE BALLAD OF KINTILLO

The Ballad of Kintillo

by Sally Rena

THE BOBBS-MERRILL COMPANY, INC.
INDIANAPOLIS / NEW YORK

Published in Great Britain by Weidenfeld and Nicolson Limited
All rights reserved, including the right of reproduction
in whole or in part in any form
Published by the Bobbs-Merrill Company, Inc.
Indianapolis   New York
ISBN 0-672-52108-3
Library of Congress catalog card number 74-21151
Designed by Ingrid Beckman
Manufactured in the United States of America

First printing

For my husband, my sons and my daughters

Kintillo is cut off from Wester Ross by high ridges of sandstone that rise up like a wall against the mainland and slope down on the southern side into the sea. One road goes over the summit of these hills, and, so long as the snow lasts, Kintillo is an island. When the spring comes, the pass is cut up with streams, and the mists settle down on the heights for days at a time. Even in the summer, there are scarcely three days together when the sky is clear, when the puddles dry up in the ruts of the road and when the mountain streams are quiet.

When the weather is warm enough the women of Kintillo village take out their kitchen chairs and sit by the sea wall. They carry their knitting with them and cups of tea, so that even though they are sitting in the sun their hands and mouths are busy. Depending on the angle of the kitchen chairs, there is a view of the whole bay, the lodge gates to Kintillo House, and the rectory on its hump of hill beyond, and no one can drive down the road from the pass without being noticed and discussed.

When the women go back across the road to cook the midday meal or when they leave their chairs to go shouting over the wall where the children are playing on the beach, the chairs are left in a semicircle like a courtroom adjourned. And this clique of women is a constant reminder of a certain scandal, five years ago, in which one man lost his mind and another died.

From the beginning of July, that summer, until the end of August, the weather was unusually hot, and almost no rain fell. The crops of barley and spring wheat grew on thin soil in the valley, and without water they sprang up in thin irregular tufts, and the grain in the husks was as small and hard as stones. The drainage ditches on the moors dried up, and the sheep came down to the peat loch Doonican, where many of them drowned in the mud on the stagnant shores. In this abnormal heat there was too much quarreling in the airless evenings, and several unwanted babies were conceived among the three villages of the peninsula.

The weather was blamed for everything, and most of all for the tragedy which followed; but the truth was simply a set of coincidences—like seeds blown in on the wind that landed on the same patch of ground and became entangled when they started to grow.

The trouble that year began with the dying of Father Macabe, the Catholic priest. Father Macabe was a dull man. When he preached the Sunday sermon the babies in the congregation began to cry. The small children sucked the tops of the church pews and crawled about under the seats. And a restless tension set in among the adults, who yawned and swatted at the children with their prayer books. When Father Macabe paid a call on his parishioners, the minute he was in the door most of them remembered several things that urgently had to be done; and while he was there they would be getting up and down in their chairs, practically dusting under his feet or doing the weekly accounts in front of him. Even those people who had plenty to complain about became dissatisfied after half an hour of uninterrupted moaning, because he was certain to agree with everything they said, and he would stare at them with his wet brown eyes until the last of the homemade scones was eaten and the teapot was empty. For eight years Father Macabe served the parishes of Kintillo and Stromeferry with as much effect as a stone embedded in a stream—he was worn away by his work, but no one noticed until the day he left for a week's holiday and did not come back.

The next Sunday, Father Lanni drove across the pass from Dornie, forty miles to the south, to say Mass and hear confessions. After the Mass was ended he leaned one hand against the edge of the pulpit and fiddled with the notes on the lectern. He cleared his throat and stared out across the heads of the congregation.

"Dearly beloved brethren," he said, "your prayers are asked for your parish priest Father Macabe, at present gravely ill."

Directly the church doors had opened, Father Lanni drove off in a great hurry back to Dornie, as though the cares of these two positions pursued him. But Father Macabe became a hero. In the following weeks the details of his illness were put together in whispers and sentences half finished, and only one thing was certain among the tangle of rumors—Father Macabe was dying and would not come back to Kintillo. The tumor in his stomach had been removed, but others grew up like knots in a heavy chain that stretched from his lungs to his intestines, and though these details were often discussed, the word cancer was never mentioned. It was like a spell cast on the minds of children.

But Father Macabe did come back, one hot close day at the end of June when the sea lay as heavy as oil in the bay and the birds were quiet on the shore. As the taxi passed by up the beach road, there were the usual numbers of women and children staring out from the cottage doors, and the same number of dogs chased the car across the bay—the dogs were luckier than the women and children, for they must have seen the dying priest clearly in every detail, although they came back to lie in the shade as if nothing had happened. For two days no one went near the rectory, and Father Macabe was nursed alone by his housekeeper.

Father Macabe was neither a landowner nor a peasant—he came from the middle classes of Aberdeen, and his only intimate friend was Father Lanni from Dornie. Besides, what can be said to a man who is dying when every word uttered reminds him of the good things in the life he is leaving behind? So out of shyness the village people left him alone, and only from time to time in the course of those three days did a few of them look up at the rectory on its hill across the bay and think they understood why he had come back. From the rectory windows the dying priest could see the great peaks of the Cuillins rising from the soft coast hills across the water. When he had pain to fight he could do it without distraction in the vast silence of an empty land, and when he died, the people of the villages believed that his soul, like theirs, would be carried out to sea on bars of light, one after another, toward the setting sun.

On the third night after Father Macabe returned, the brazen Murdo Mackenzie went up the hill to call on him with the small pretext of crab-apple jam as a present. By the time he had been up there an hour, most of the village knew where he was; the pub was full, and the crowd that had gathered overflowed into the street and across it by the sea wall. There was nothing whatsoever to do but drink. The air inside the pub was stifling with smoke and stale beer, and outside the night was as cold as April without a stir of wind. There were times, that summer, when the twilight seemed to linger on too long. Flecks of the night as thick as moths began to gather in the air, the land and the sky began to merge, and still there was light enough to see by. When Murdo Mackenzie came back down the hill, he was pale and distorted by the coming night, and his body seemed to float above the ground. There was a hush among the people standing around the pub door as they listened to the sound of his footsteps in the shadows of the village street, and the atmosphere of the evening, which had been bored and slack, tightened like a trip wire. Murdo seemed to swell with importance as he came into the light, and though the bottom half of his face was solemn and sad, his eyes shone with excitement.

No one spoke. His cousin bought him a drink, and small groups of men broke up and came over casually to where he stood. Murdo drank the whole pint of beer and wiped his mouth with the back of his hand. Presently he stared in a sad way at the dregs in his mug and hitched at the string around his trouser tops with his free hand. No one moved.

Finally his cousin said, "Well, how is he, then? Since you're waiting to tell us."

"Terrible," Murdo said, "just terrible."

He put down the beer mug on the top of the sea wall and steadied it carefully so it should not fall off, and then he began to speak.

"When I came in the room," he said, "there was just this candle burning by the bed. There was this bitter smell—medicines, jars of all sorts, and Father Macabe was lying quite still there in the bed." He gazed at the light that hung above the pub door. A few moths flickered about the light, and Murdo squinted his eyes and spoke with his voice a little lifted. "As true as I'm standing here," he went on, "he was lying so still I thought the poor man was already gone. His eyes hung loose in the sockets ready to fall out and his hands were spread out stiff on the covers."

Although it was unfortunate to have to listen to him bragging about the suffering of Father Macabe, nobody moved away.

"I put the pot of jam down on the bedside table," said

Murdo, "and I went to sit down by the bed where he could see me plainly in the light. At that he moved a little, and he asked me in a whisper to wet his lips, for his throat was dry. When I'd done this, he was able to speak quite clearly and asked after my family and the relatives—but he had something on his mind, agitating him—and after a bit he began to describe to me what they did to him in the hospital."

Murdo still spoke in a grave, slow voice, but he raised it a little so that those who had just then come out of the pub could hear him clearly.

"They removed," he said, "a growth the size and shape of a pineapple from the wall of his stomach. They operated on him maybe three times in the next few weeks, and each time there was another one, bigger and more terrible than the rest. By the time they had done with him, most of his insides were gone and his suffering was terrible. Sometimes while he was speaking I had to get up from the chair and wipe the perspiration from his forehead, for it was rolling into his eyes. And then toward the end of his stay in the hospital, he would keep nothing down and was fainting from the pain. There was nothing left to be done but to ring up his mother in Aberdeen and prepare her for the death . . ."

At the bold use of the word death, several of those who had been listening most closely began to move away and to pay more attention to their drinks. And though Murdo went on elaborating on the sufferings of the priest, the thread of attention had snapped. It was cold outside. The night had finally come and with it a mean little wind that blew dust and bits of rubbish along the street, and most of Murdo's audience were suddenly anxious to get back inside the pub. From the shadows just inside the pub door a clear sad voice rose up. The lobsterman Danny started singing, some nights when it was getting late and he was drunk, the Song of the

Summer Isles. He had never been there, but he sang with such infinite longing that for many people who listened the Summer Isles were Paradise, a place they had believed in when they were children and never found in all the years afterward. But that particular night, as the lobsterman went home, balancing gently against the houses and tripping over the doorsteps, he went on singing. His voice trailed out behind him and remained in the minds of the people who followed him, a lament for Father Macabe.

Murdo Mackenzie stood and watched Danny go by, with his arms slack by his sides and a queer look of shame on his face, and once or twice before he left the pub he glanced up to the point where the rectory stood on the hills and looked away again quickly.

The following morning, before the village shop was open, Miss Morag, the priest's housekeeper, came running down the beach road as fast as her clumsy legs would take her. Her face in the morning light was a sickly yellow, and her story was repeated several times before it made any sense. It seemed that when Murdo Mackenzie had walked up to the rectory the evening before in the twilight, perhaps to do with the staring face of Miss Morag in the doorway, and perhaps to do with the cramped darkness in the rectory hall, he had taken fright. He had thrust the pot of crab-apple jam into her hands and rushed out the back way, stumbling over the coal scuttle in the kitchen and knocking the lid off the dustbin outside. He had sat for an hour on the shoulder of the hill, never moving except to light a cigarette, and all this time Miss Morag had watched him until he came back through the shadows of the sycamores and set off down the road to the pub.

As near as she was able to judge in her loose-witted way, about the time that Murdo fell over the coal scuttle by the kitchen range, Father Macabe had died.

It was a part of that strange summer that the death of the priest was like a stone flung into a stagnant pond, from which the waves spread out across the whole peninsula. In the pubs of Kintillo, Toscaig, and Camusrury, the patrons sat subdued, discussing the suddenness and terror of such a death. And while they drank their beer with whisky chasers, the women sat at home in the long evenings, knitting together in twos and threes and elaborating on the suffering of Father Macabe.

His body was taken away to be buried in Aberdeen, and the shutters were closed on all the rectory windows that faced the bay. From the village below, the house had a queer blank look, like an idiot face that is crazed with grief, and when the long twilight began, it shone strangely in the dusk and could still be seen long after the shoulder of the hill behind it had melted into the night.

Inside the rectory, now that the priest was dead, his housekeeper ate and slept when she pleased. Often she did not bother to get dressed. She walked about the darkened rooms in an old overcoat that she wore as a dressing gown, and when she was hungry she made herself cups of sweet tea and cut slices from a Dundee cake that she had bought for Father Macabe before he died. She kept the kitchen range stoked up with fuel, and she sat by the kitchen table stirring the cups of tea until they were almost cold. Occasionally a tea leaf floated to the top of the cup, and she fished it out with a spoon and slapped it against the back of her hand, counting the days until a handsome stranger would come to the door. Whenever she thought of the handsome stranger she began to laugh, and the sound of this laughter was high and disconnected in the silence of the house.

She took leisurely walks about the house, watching the dust build up on the woodwork and dropping the crumbs of her Dundee cake on the bare floorboards. The dust floated up and down the sunbeams between the shutters and settled on the furniture. She watched its progress from day to day, and still there was no sign of the new parish priest.

From the kitchen she looked out through the sycamore trees toward the church. Close to the kitchen window the parish car was parked. It was so old and dilapidated that someday it would break down on the steep flanks of the pass and refuse to move again. At such a thought, Morag would smile to herself.

Twice she heard the church bell ringing for Mass on a Sunday morning, and twice she was dressed and sitting at the kitchen table waiting for Father Lanni to come to the rectory door. She would sit there without moving for almost an hour until she heard the congregation leaving the church at the end of Mass. Then she would get up from her chair and open the shutter a little to watch for the priest coming out of the church. For two Sundays Father Lanni came down the cinder path from the vestry in a great hurry and climbed into his car without once glancing toward the rectory. Miss Morag closed the shutter again and celebrated those Sundays with an extra helping of food. By the third week, however, there was a single handful of dusty lentils at the bottom of a sack and the last of the porridge oats simmered in a pot on the range. There were even times in the dark silence of the empty house when she felt sure that the new priest would never come. On those days she strolled about freely, humming a certain tuneless song, and she would help herself to the drink that was locked in a cupboard under the stairs. She was sitting one afternoon in Father Macabe's chair by the study fire staring at the sunlight through the shutters—if she shut one eye hard and then the other, the light jumped sharply across the lino floor. She had a glass of sherry balanced on the arm of the chair and was raising the remains to her mouth when the front doorbell rang. She stopped with the glass halfway to her lips and waited for the bell to ring again.

Father Lanni began to beat on the rectory door with his fist and to rattle the doorknob. When her brain started working again Miss Morag was out of her chair with great speed. She hid the sherry glass behind the coal scuttle, tightened the belt of the overcoat sharply, and reached the front door just as Father Lanni had his finger on the bell for the second time.

"Ah, Miss Morag?" he said. "I was beginning to think the bell was out of order—"

He stopped and stared at her. She was blinking in the sudden light and her face was pale and dirty.

"Are you ill?" he said. "Is anything the matter with you?"

"You'll be wanting to come in, then," she said. She moved back into the shadows of the hall. "I'll have to fix the shutters."

She went ahead of him through the study door, and while he hesitated in the unaccustomed darkness she had time to hide the sherry bottle behind the big armchair, and she threw the shutters back with a clatter against the walls.

"I can't stay long," Father Lanni said. "I was up administering the last rites to Mrs. Mackenzie at the Dower Farm."

He sat down with a sigh in Father Macabe's armchair and wiped his forehead with the back of his hand.

"I could do with a little refreshment," he said. "With my weight I suffer greatly from the heat."

Miss Morag watched him with her arms folded and her back to the light.

"There's no' much in the house," she said without moving. "The rations is all used up."

She disliked Father Lanni for two reasons. He spoke slowly to her as if he were dealing with a backward child, and while some people ignored her walleye or looked away, Father Lanni made an effort to stare her in the face in the same bold way he might have stared at a hunchback, to show that he was not afraid.

"Now, Miss Morag," he said playfully, "considering I have come up here to the rectory to see how you're getting on, I think I'm entitled to a cup of tea."

"As you wish," she said, shrugging. The light hurt her eyes—it pressed down on the lids and made her dizzy.

"I'll away and make it, then," she said.

Father Lanni lay back in the chair and yawned, and when she came in with the tea tray his mouth was half open and his hands were folded loosely on his heavy stomach.

"There's no milk," she said, setting down the tray.

Father Lanni straightened himself up and sighed.

"Now look here, my good woman," he said, pouring out the tea, "you will have to pull yourself together a bit before Father James arrives. Considering there are many people who would like a nice comfortable job like this . . ." He put three lumps of sugar in the cup and stirred it thoroughly.

"It won't do," he continued. "You have a nice respectable position here. Father James is a young man. He will certainly like things nicely done. He comes from the south, you understand, from England, and they are very particular there about cleanliness and so forth. . . ."

"Father James," she said. "That's a funny name."

She stood in front of the old priest with her arms folded and a sour expression on her face.

"It's a funny name," she said again.

Father Lanni shook his head and made a clicking noise with his tongue. He finished his tea in a hurry. The atmosphere in the room was warm and stale and the dust in his nostrils gave him an urge to sneeze.

"Now you be thinking about what I said." He pulled

himself slowly out of the chair and straightened the creases in his cassock. "It's your Christian duty to have the place cleaned up and ready within the week."

By the study door he turned and looked at her severely.

"It was a beautiful Mass we had last Sunday for Father Macabe," he said. "I was disappointed not to see you there, Miss Morag."

For a moment she looked afraid. She pulled the old overcoat tightly around her body and cradled herself with her bony hands.

"I couldn't go," she said. "I was sick."

He looked at her a little longer; then he sighed and spoke carefully, separating each word from the next.

"I am bringing Father James from the three o'clock train next Tuesday. We shall be here about five. I should like everything ready for him, you understand; otherwise, I shall have to take steps," he said firmly. "I shall have to speak to the bishop."

He watched her while she took this in. She ran her tongue over her lips and shifted her gaze to the floor.

"It'll be done," she said, nodding. "He won't need to complain."

She saw that he was satisfied with that. He turned and went out into the hall, fussing with the belt of his cassock and preparing himself to face the heat again. Miss Morag watched him from the shadows when he climbed into his car. She slammed the door behind him and waited until she heard him drive away, and then she walked into the study and smashed his teacup on the floor. She stamped on the broken cup until it was shattered into small fragments, and then she went slowly to the kitchen and fetched a dustpan and brush. She swept up the pieces carefully and sponged down the lino floor, and by the time the sun had set that evening she had cleaned out every room; she had polished the furniture and dusted all the pictures, and finally she opened the shutters and the windows wide. The sounds of the warm night came drifting back from the valley and the hillside, and these sounds tormented her like the pieces of a half-heard song that she could no longer put together.

Morag was walleyed and ugly, and the hair grew on her head in thin irregular tufts which resembled the down on a newborn baby's scalp. Throughout the peninsula she was treated as a harmless joke.

There was a certain ballad, sung in the pubs late at night to the beating of fists upon the bar. It began with the legend of Morag's mother, Roving Mary, and of the unknown sailor who had fathered her sixty years before. Various verses were added to it from one year to the next, and it was known throughout the peninsula as the Ballad of Morag Anon. There were certain odd gaps in it where the singers had forgotten the facts, and sometimes an incident was invented to add more interest to it. For the truth of Morag's life was simple, uneventful, and often sad.

After Roving Mary was sent away from Kintillo, Lady Finlay brought up Mary's daughter to be kitchen maid in her place. She was dressed in castoff clothes and sent to the village school where she learned neither to read nor to write, and she grew up to peel potatoes and sweep out the kitchens of Kintillo House. She scoured the range and took the pails of pig swill down to the home farm, and when her work was done she would sit dumbly in a chair for hours at a time, and her odd eyes would flitter about the room like restless birds that had nowhere to alight.

Succeeding cooks complained about her, saying that she worked too slowly and without any system, so that when Morag was nearly thirty, Lady Finlay took her up the road to the rectory, where the post of housekeeper had fallen vacant. She never left again. For a long time she worked with a dim sadness settling over everything she did. She looked sometimes from the study window, out across the bay, and her eyes would fill with tears, although she had no idea why she was crying.

When Father Macabe came to Kintillo he treated her kindly. He listened when she spoke to him, and he never finished a sentence for her nor hurried her through one. The little religion she had scraped together was lifted from his sermons on a Sunday morning. She fell in love with him, and this love, like an unaccustomed warmth after a long winter spread throughout her body and gave a peculiar brightness to her one blue eye.

One day Father Macabe asked her to come into the study and sit across from him in an armchair. He had never done this before, and Morag sat down uneasily and gazed at the floor in front of her. While the priest was speaking she became more and more absorbed by the pattern in the carpet that stretched between them. And afterward she could only think of his coming death clearly when she remembered the ugly floral design, as if the greater of the two realities was this.

For the next three days she stayed in her room, and the priest had to cook for himself. Occasionally he leaned against her door and asked her to come out, altering the tone of his voice in various ways to try to move her. When he listened closely he heard nothing, but at night when he lay in bed he could hear through the walls a high thin keening like the howling of an animal whose master has left it. When her elected time of mourning was over, Morag never cried again, not even on the day he died. And when the undertakers came she looked indifferently at his corpse before it was put into the coffin, and walked across the passage to her room.

In a box there, she kept the few things he had given her: a wooden rosary, a child's prayer book, and some postcards he had sent her from Aberdeen. Sometimes, when her memories of him became vague or confused, she would open this box and run her hands lightly over the objects inside it. In this way she was able to remember again exactly how he was.

She hated the new priest with a profound intensity. She had hated him some time before she ever met him.

2

And it won't be easy," Father Lanni was saying again. "I'm afraid it won't be easy at all."

"I didn't expect—"

"And the thing you have to remember—have some more tea—is that these people are scarcely Christians. Consider the mission of Saint Iona in the fourth century. Large parts of this coast were converted to Catholicism and many of them have remained so ever since—but do you think this is out of a sense of conviction?"

"Yes, I believe they—"

"Well, it's nothing of the sort. If the Protestant reformers had made an effort to reach these coasts, they could have converted whole areas to the Church of Scotland. The religion here is entirely superficial—basically they are all pagans, complete pagans."

Father James let him talk. Since he had arrived half an hour ago in the rectory, and indeed since he had left the station in Fort William, the new priest had scarcely been able to open his mouth. Father Lanni had lived so long alone that it was impossible for him to listen to anyone else without becoming restless and uneasy.

"They are pagan by character, you see, as well as by tradition. Because they live mostly from the land and above all from the sea, the seasons, the climate—these things affect them far more than anything we can impose upon them in the way of discipline. Basically, you see—"

While he was talking, Father James murmured and nodded now and then, and looked about the room. The rectory study was small and dark, overshadowed by the trees outside the window: from where he sat he could see nothing but the sky imprisoned there and a small patch of leaves moving silently in the slight wind, up and down the same windowpane. Inside the room the paint on the walls had turned yellow with age and the woodwork was varnished brown. There were patches of damp around the skirting boards and in the corners of the ceiling. And all these things, even the worn-out lino and the dingy rug in front of the fireplace, were identical to those in the rectory he had left five hours ago in Lennoxtown.

Father Lanni was finishing the buttered bread and filling up the teapot again.

"—and there was another thing I meant to discuss with you which I almost forgot. I daresay you have been worrying about Miss Morag, the housekeeper . . ."

Father James smiled. "Not at all," he said. "She seems perfect—no one will gossip about us, will they, up here on the hill together alone."

"I don't think you take my point," Father Lanni said heavily. "I daresay you haven't had time to notice her—well, her manner."

"Oh, yes," said Father James gently. "I should imagine she's quite simple-minded, but that doesn't worry me, you know. We shan't see very much of each other, and I'm sure she does her work very well or she—"

"Yes—well, if it really doesn't worry you."

Father Lanni was uneasy. He felt that the conversation was only half-finished; there were essential points in it that he hadn't developed yet, but Father James had a curious way of speaking that was light and at the same time solemn. The old priest couldn't pin it down—if he had been able to put it into words he would have said that he resembled a man who was pursuing a certain dream in which both the time and the place had been chosen long ago. He sat for a little in silence, stirring his cup of tea, and Father James sat watching him.

"Have you been here long at Dornie?"

"Yes, a long time now—a very long time. I took over the parish there at the same time that Father Macabe came here."

"You must miss him, then. I'm sorry."

"I miss his company," said Father Lanni. He felt the return of an old grievance. "You don't get much civilized company around here," he added. "They're a lazy lot—no interest in anything, you see, no curiosity—I mean intellectual curiosity, you understand. Most of them are quite content to live out their lives catching a few fish, poaching salmon, growing a few turnips and potatoes and of course drinking . . ."

"They must be very poor," Father James said.

"Poor. They don't try. Do you realize no one has made the slightest effort to drain the land, apart from the valley, of course. There are whole acres of the hillside around here that could be planted with trees. Forestry brings in a nice income. But no one does a thing. I am constantly exhorting them from the pulpit. There are plenty of examples throughout the country of flourishing communities, growing populations, and so forth, under exactly the same conditions. . . ."

"But surely it's the landowner's—"

"Under exactly the same conditions—and if you think I haven't told them. But it's always the same. They complain that the population is decreasing, and I tell them over and over again if only . . . but it's no use talking." Father Lanni tugged angrily at his dog collar and rose suddenly to his feet.

"Here," he said, "I'll show you. Come outside a minute."

He took the young priest by the arm and dragged him to the door.

"I'll show you what I mean," he said. "I'll show you just what I mean."

Outside, a warm south wind was blowing across the valley and the air was full of light. Father James shut his eyes and let the sun shine full in his face. On his own he might have walked down to the beach for a while where the tide was going out and the sands stretched clear to the mouth of the bay. But Father Lanni was still holding on to him and was shouting in his ear.

"And over there," he was saying, pointing up the hillside, "is a perfect example. Wasted land . . . two hundred acres at least . . . completely going to waste—"

The wind blew his voice away and Father James no longer listened. He looked down across the bay. The village of Kintillo faced north among the hollows of Ben Beann. There was a line of white cottages above the beach, a high wood, a few fields, and a one-track road going south to Camusrury and Toscaig. The mountains of Torridon rose up in a circle to the north and east, and to the west, across the sea, the ragged lines of the Cuillins were black against the evening sky.

"And do you realize," cried Father Lanni, "you can't even grow runner beans here? And do you know why not? The light, there's not enough light. In the winter after two o'clock in the afternoon it's dark, completely dark." As he spoke his face was now so close to Father James that a glob of spit hit the young priest on the cheek.

"I think we'd better go in," he said gloomily. "It's almost time for supper. Though considering the kind of food—"

He released Father James's arm at last and they went back into the house.

"It will certainly be mutton," he said as they sat down for the evening meal. He spread out his napkin carefully on his knees. "I can guarantee it'll be mutton. When I think eight years back to the time I arrived in Dornie, we used to get good meat then, straight from the local markets. Rump steak, wing rib, even occasionally a nice leg of pork. And now what do you think they cook? Scotch broth, lentil soup, mashed turnips. When I think . . . There, you see—good evening, Miss Morag. That looks delicious."

Miss Morag came in with a bowl of brown soup and pushed the door shut with her bottom. She nodded at the priests, put down the plates and soup tureen on the side table, and left.

"After you," said Father Lanni. "You must do the honors, considering that this is now your parish."

Father James smiled absentmindedly. He felt unable to make any effort. His head had begun to ache and he felt very tired. Nothing was the way he had imagined it. He had thought about this place for so long, planned what he would do and prayed for it. And now that he was here he felt only exhaustion. The old priest's conversation tightened around him like a web—there were hundreds of invisible threads which tied him down and prevented him from thinking clearly about anything. He kept saying to himself, "I have done nothing; I have been here for three hours and I have done nothing." He suddenly realized that he had eaten half his meal without seeing or tasting a single mouthful. Father Lanni was leaning forward asking him something. He was rolling up pieces of bread in his thick fingers, and the crumbs were scattered around his plate.

"And you won't mind my saying this, I hope—I mean since we've only just met—"

"I'm sorry. I wasn't listening. What is it?"

"But they aren't—I mean the parish—they won't be expecting you—someone like you, you see. . . ."

Father James was surprised.

"I don't understand. I'm just an ordinary parish priest. From what you said I thought they weren't really interested in me—"

Father Lanni swayed anxiously in his chair.

"No, no, you misunderstood me, no—these things affect them deeply. I mean, changes in the community—such a small enclosed community as this—no, they are vitally concerned, you see, but the thing is—I don't know how to put it . . ."

"Because I'm English, you mean—they might find me odd. Perhaps they won't understand the way I speak. Do they resent the English?"

"Oh, no, no, no, not that—well, perhaps a little, but no . . ." The old man became agitated. Crumbs bounced off his cassock, and he flapped at them with clumsy fingers. The expression on his face was at once sly and embarrassed.

"Forgive me, Father James," he said, leaning forward in his chair, "but you look—well, you see, for this kind of parish . . . now you won't take offense, will you? You see, you are too young and really too, er—different. . . ." He was disconcerted.

Father James began to laugh. The knife and fork he was holding slipped from his hands and fell to the floor. He bent to pick them up, and afterward his face was flushed with embarrassment.

"I'm sorry," he said. "I didn't mean to laugh. That was rude of me. But you reminded me of my Father Administrator. He gave me the same warning just a little while ago. He was very much against my coming here. I think that if he could have sent anyone else, I should never have been considered. He warned me against the isolation and the loneliness. He said that I shouldn't last out the year in such a place." He smiled. "But it was the way he speaks, like a man rewriting the Bible. He said, 'Small flocks have sharp eyes.' I think that was just what you meant, wasn't it?"

"Well, yes—in effect—yes."

Father Lanni was now uncomfortable. He became shy and vague. "Yes, well . . . it won't be easy for you, then. You see, they will be naturally suspicious—for this reason it won't be easy."

He shook his head slowly. He was conscious of coming around in a full circle upon himself. "Tell me about your last parish," he said suddenly.

They ate trifle from little glass dishes that were chipped and gray. The trifle was pasty and insipid, but Father Lanni finished his rapidly and licked the spoon until it was clean.

"I gather you had no holiday between these two posts."

"No—things happened in the end so quickly, there was no time. I wish, in a way, that I had. I should have liked to go home for a while. I come from a large family, you know. So much seems to happen there without being organized, and I love that—the noise and the chaos—I'm used to it. The dogs cover the sofas with hair, the rabbits escape from their hutches and nest in the drawing room, and sometimes," he said, laughing, "we have no joint for Sunday lunches—the dogs get into the larder and eat it."

Father Lanni laughed too, but he stopped almost immediately.

"I'm afraid you will find it very dull here," he said repressively. "Very dull indeed."

"Oh, no," Father James said, leaning forward quickly. "You don't understand. I want—"

But what it was he wanted he never said. Suddenly he stopped speaking and flushed. When he flushed his eyes watered with embarrassment. He had eyes of a deep, strong blue; the lids were heavy and finely shaped and the eyelashes long and curved, and when he was excited the irises darkened until they were almost black and shone with a strange intensity. The old man pursed his lips and sighed. Certainly, Father James had never been troubled by loneliness in his life. Fresh from a university or a seminary—it made no difference—he was the same bright-faced and hopeless idealist that Father Lanni had often seen before.

"I'm sorry," Father James was saying. "It's very difficult for me to explain why I wanted to come here. You see, to do that I would have to—it's very personal—it's part of a"— he meant to say "a dream," but once again he stopped himself, sighed, and began again. "I was going to tell you about my last parish, wasn't I?" He smiled, and this smile lit up the whole of his face.

Oh, he has charm, Father Lanni thought. Oh, he has that all right—but it's the wrong kind of behavior for this place. He's an intellectual—imagine sending an intellectual like that here.

"Lennoxtown, wasn't it?" he said. "A very large busy parish, that. I haven't been down to that part of Scotland recently—Glasgow I know, you understand . . . but Lennoxtown, I never had the opportunity of going there . . . a very prosperous busy parish, I've heard, though; plenty going on, and so forth."

"Well, yes," said Father James politely. "I suppose some of the things we managed to get done—but on the whole I thought the place was so poor I wondered how we should—"

"Poor!" Father Lanni cried. "You should see the squalor that some of the people around here live in—not fit for pigs, mind you, and do you think I can get them to take an interest or a pride in themselves, considering the time I have spent. . . ."

Father James pressed his hands hard together in his lap. It was useless to argue. Everything returned to the same point; like a merry-go-round at a fair, the conversation went up and down, up and down, but always in the same circle and at the same speed. He remembered his first few days in Lennoxtown—his first parish. He had been so proud, so full of enthusiasm; he had walked from one end of the town to the other—and found every street the same. The air was bitter from the smell of the tanning factory, and a constant wind blew around the corners, a sad wind from the Campsie fells, full of grit and empty paper bags. The town was empty— there was nothing to do there, and the mods and rockers polished their motorbikes and drove off to Glasgow on Saturday nights, where the poverty was noisy and real and the streets were neon-lit.

He had done nothing there—nothing that he really wanted to do.

"Perhaps we should go next door," he said, getting to his feet. "I didn't realize how late it was getting—I still haven't unpacked yet or done anything—"

"Ah, yes," said Father Lanni. "One forgets, what with the long twilights we get here." He folded his napkin neatly and rose from the table, staggering a little under his own weight. In the narrow hallway, practically pressed against Father Lanni's stomach, the young priest said good night.

"I hope you'll forgive me," he said. "I have so much to do upstairs—I think I should get everything sorted out—my books and things. . . ."

"Go ahead, my son. I understand," Father Lanni said. He ran a finger around the inside of his mouth where a piece of food was lodged. "I shall go to bed myself soon. I don't sit around very late in the evenings as a rule."

Father James watched him go slowly into the study. He felt guilty. The old man must have spent many evenings by the fireside with Father Macabe. And on those evenings there had been someone to listen to him while he talked, a little drink to warm him before he went to bed, and the sound of someone moving about in another room when he turned out the light to go to sleep.

I should go in there and sit with him again, he thought. He shut his eyes and leaned against the cool bannisters. Somewhere at the base of his skull a headache was spreading out, like the tendrils of some poisonous plant which prevented him from thinking clearly about anything.

"I must go and unpack," he said aloud, but almost immediately he changed his mind. He opened the front door quietly and walked out into the night.

The days in Kintillo are long and wax-yellow in midsummer, and you can read a book out of doors until eleven o'clock on a warm evening. The stillness is so complete that if a child cries out or a door slams across the water in the village, it can be clearly heard from the rectory garden, and it leaves a space behind it in the night. Father James walked up the shoulder of the hill on a little path which ran through the trees behind the house. He walked quickly and noiselessly. Halfway up the hill, however, he stumbled on a sharp piece of rock, and a few stones rattled loose down the steep slope behind him. He turned around sharply as though he expected to see Father Lanni come out from the shadows of the house and look up the hill toward him. There was nothing. The silence was so deep that he could hear the sound of his own breathing. Then he noticed, in a back window on the first floor of the rectory, a face pressed against the windowpane, staring directly toward him in the dusk. He had the strange impression that Miss Morag had watched him, motionless, since he left the house and that she would go on staring at him with the same terrible attentiveness until he was out of sight over the lip of the hill.

He walked on until he lost the path among some rocks and the rectory was far below him in the hollow. He was quite alone on the bare mountain side. Above him the ground stretched up to a sharp skyline, and beyond it on the other side he knew there was nothing for thirty-five miles along the coast but the ruins of deserted crofts and the empty wastes of the moors. Down in the bay the sea was calm and the tiny village of Kintillo hung to the far shore like a cluster of pebbles that sooner or later the tide would wash away. He sat for a long time on the shoulder of the hill, watching the light fade and thicken on the water and the shadows change slowly from gray to black.

Ten years ago on a similar night in summer, he had decided to become a priest. But the nights in the South of England had a different feeling to them. Although the splendor was missing from them, in its place there were the numberless soft sounds, the stirring of leaves and grass, and the movement of a small night world along the hedges and in the woods around his house. And down by the river while he was fishing, the sky was a pale apple green by half past eight and dark by nine o'clock.

He could no longer remember when the idea to become a priest had first occurred to him, and for a while he had ignored it. He would get up in the mornings thinking, There is something disagreeable I have to do today, and then he would remember what it was. For the spring of one year and half the summer, he refused to give in to it. He was in love with his cousin Alice at the time, and this love was absurd and painful. He watched her and could not touch her. He was tormented by her indifference, and yet there was something delightful about this torment. It was intolerable that he should be asked to give it up; to give it up, moreover, for a life of chastity and uncompromising belief that was cold and repulsive to him.

He went to France, in the beginning of that July, with his brother Michael and a friend, and when they reached Paris they decided to stay there instead of going on to the Auvergne, as they had planned. For ten days and nights they wasted their money among the bars and small nightclubs on the Left Bank. Frequently they ate nothing in the mornings, nor at lunchtime either, so that this money could be spent on cheap wine, small dingy floor shows, and finally on prostitutes. Some of these experiences were delightful, and others, for no reason, pointless and sad. And presently they began to find, each of them without telling the others, that whole evenings had passed which they could not remember. It was as if they had paid their money at the door to see a show and had walked instead into some strange uneasy darkness.

Two days after he returned home, he went down to the river to fish. He had two things on his mind. First, there was his faithlessness to his cousin Alice, which he now considered with a certain guilty pleasure, and then there was another feeling which he could not put into words. For a long time now he had been in a state of indecision. He would decide to become a lawyer one day and then a teacher the next. Or he would decide he was going to University, and then gradually forget the idea, finding it a waste of time. He would begin to study something that interested him, collect together any number of books on the subject; but when the time came for him to start on it, he would abandon the whole idea and go out to a party instead. Finally that evening, by the river bank, while he was standing there half-hypnotized by the water's movements, he saw clearly that all these fine thoughts and ideals amounted to as little as a hill of beans.

He was only eighteen. He had time to make up his mind about what he wanted to do. But the idea was already there, and not merely there, but clear to him in every detail. Almost with relief he had returned to it, and he was surprised to discover that somehow it suited him. Going home through the dark fields, he walked slowly, almost in a dream. Once he said to himself aloud, "I'm going to become a priest," and immediately he smiled, for the words no longer sounded strange to him.

Father James gazed out across the bay. Ben Beann was still visible against the night sky, and beyond it the clear lines of the coast spread out to the south, one dark ridge after another going down into the sea. Although his eyes took in these things, in his mind he could see another valley, the broad valley of the Thames, the streets of a busy city, and the pale stone cloisters of the Oxford Seminary. He had spent seven years in Oxford, and now those years had shortened themselves into a single memory of intense happiness.

Suddenly a bird cried out behind him on the hill. He realized that he was cold and that the night had finally come. He got up stiffly from the rock he had been sitting on and started back down the path toward the rectory.

3

When he came down the next morning Father Lanni was already eating breakfast. He was finishing a boiled egg. In spite of the clean way he had cut off the top of it, and in spite of the napkin tucked into his collar, he had managed to spill some egg yolk on the cuff of his cassock.

"Good morning to you," he said as the new priest came in. "I hope you slept well, my son. It's a strange thing, though, considering that I like to get about a bit and have a change now and then, I can never sleep well in an unfamiliar room. And then, of course, though I don't mean to depress you, the food here—I had terrible indigestion last night. . . ."

While he was getting dressed, Father James had thought of a number of things to ask the old priest about his new parish. But now, when he sat down opposite him and began to eat his breakfast, he found that he had forgotten half of them, and that the rest seemed scarcely worth mentioning.

He poured himself a cup of tea. "It's another beautiful day," he said.

"This weather is unnatural, however," said Father Lanni. "You know, we are having a drought here."

"Yes, I did hear something about it. I heard there might have to be some kind of water rationing."

"Huh, well, that kind of thing will never get organized around here. Such a notion is completely foreign to these people. Economy is something they have never understood; they are born wasters—"

Father James interrupted him quickly. "I know what I wanted to ask you," he said. "I was wondering if you could go through the parish register with me. I was hoping you might be able to sort out the various families a little. For instance, I know there are a great number of Mackenzies and also Macleods. Perhaps with your help I should get a better feeling of the place. . . ."

Father Lanni was gazing at him again with a faded stare. "Well," he said, "I haven't much time—"

"Oh, I know, I do appreciate—"

"Not at all. I don't get much civilized company—it's a real pleasure to be here. But I must get back to my parish duties and so forth. You know how it is: when you leave other people to do the work, it never gets done. So the simplest thing would be—when you've finished your breakfast—"

"I'm ready now."

"Yes, well, the simplest thing would be if I take you down to the village now on my way home. I know they are anxious to see what—to meet you, you see, and then I really must be getting on home."

As they were ready to leave the house, the telephone rang, and Miss Morag came out of the study. Without looking at Father James, she said, "It's for you, then."

"For me?" he asked. He felt the blood rising in his face. Miss Morag went through the baize door into the kitchen without replying.

"It'll be Mr. Finlay," Father Lanni whispered suddenly in his ear.

"Who?"

"The son of the laird—you'd better go in there and speak to him quickly."

Two minutes later Father James came back. "He's asked me to dinner," he said.

"That's wonderful news," Father Lanni cried. "Wonderful

news—I was sure he would ask you. Father Macabe always dined there on Sunday nights."

"What is he like? I'm afraid I must have made a bad impression on him. He was very cold and abrupt."

"Mr. Finlay?" the old man said vaguely. He seemed at a loss to describe him. "Well, now, his life has not been easy, you see, but considering this, he is a wonderful man . . . very educated, and quite devoted to his father, of course. . . ." Charles Finlay existed in the priest's mind in the same way that a river flows down its natural course and the sun sets in the same place on the horizon. As they walked out to his car, he elaborated instead on the long and noble history of the Finlays; how it was that they had lived on the same land for four or even five centuries, and how they had bravely fought the English at the battle of Culloden Moor. As they were driving down the hill toward the village, he indicated with a sweep of his hand the size and grandeur of their Georgian house, and the old car ran over a stone in the road and swerved about. He pointed out the lodge gates through which it was believed the ghost of General Robert Finlay drove with his coach and four, on moonless nights, when the lairds of Applecross lay dying, and Father James gazed distractedly at the spot of dried egg on the cuff of Father Lanni's cassock.

Suddenly Father Lanni stopped the car in the middle of the road and climbed out. He leaned over the edge of the door.

"It's a terrible business to turn around on the sea road once you are on it. I prefer to leave my car here, where it's ready to go up the pass."

"Is it all right—in the middle of the road, I mean?"

"Nothing goes up this road," Father Lanni said simply. "You might say it's now your exclusive property. The North Lodge gates are never used, you understand. The old man, Sir John, does not go visiting, now that his wife is dead.

There is no occasion to keep up the grandeur of the past."

They began to walk up the road to the village. The wind had veered to the west, and Father Lanni's cassock billowed out gently behind him like a boat that has half caught sail.

"My, my," he said. "What beautiful weather we're having. I think I can see Angus Cameron in the village street idling around as usual . . . a perfect example of what I was telling you just now about the laziness of these people. He's twenty-six, able-bodied, perfectly intelligent, and yet I don't believe he has done a day's real work in his life. . . ."

As the two priests walked up the village street, there was a long, unnatural silence. By the sea wall, a man was mending an old Ford van. Over the upraised bonnet, though his hands were occupied, his eyes were fixed on the priests. Two children were playing beside him in the road. Their high voices broke off in midair and they too began to stare. The silence was so complete that if one of the priests had dropped a coin in the road, he would have heard it roll away into the ditch. Father James, with his very clear skin, began to blush, and he felt his hands grow soft and damp. His black cloth suit cut him off from the village people, and though Father Lanni greeted the children by name as he went past, they answered him at random, with their eyes on the new priest.

When they reached the post office, Father Lanni began talking loudly before he was halfway through the door, as though this were a prearranged signal for the people inside to straighten themselves from lounging against the counter.

The post office was dark and cramped and the air was dusty. Besides dealing with the mail, the postmistress ran a general store. The wall behind the counter was stacked to the ceiling with sacks of lentils and flour, tin boxes of biscuits, and crates of cheap soap which gave out a sour and bitter smell. The counter was crowded with jars of sweets, postcard racks, and bundles of pens and pencils tied up with elastic bands. In the middle of this confusion, like a single flower growing out of a rubbish heap, Jean Macpherson the postmistress stood. She was sorting the letters beside her on the counter, stamping them and throwing them into a mailbag on the floor. She smiled shyly at the priests and went on with her work.

"It's fine weather we're having," said Father Lanni.

"It is that," she answered. Her skin was very pale, and there were freckles on the bridge of her nose.

"Father James came down the beach road with me," he said, "to see me on my way. I thought we'd take the opportunity to call in and see you while we were passing. I told Father James you'd look after him, Jeanie, if he has any problems, you see, and with his mail and things."

There were three other men in the shop planted among the shadows. They were shifting from one foot to the other and staring at the wall behind the counter. At the mention of Father James, they felt free to stare at him for a minute before returning their gazes again to the wall.

"I should be very grateful for your help," Father James said to Jeanie.

For some reason she blushed and began to fiddle with the letters in front of her on the counter. The shop was now so quiet that the sounds coming from another room could be clearly heard and seemed oddly loud and emphatic.

"The Reverend Father," said the old priest, "has been telling me how much he admires the scenery here."

"It's your first visit, then?" Jeanie spoke softly, so that Father James had to lean forward slightly to hear her.

"Yes—I've never been to the west coast before. I think it's very beautiful."

One of the men behind him in the shadows cleared his throat. "There was a fellow up here not long ago," he began. "You remember him, Jean, from one of the big newspapers in the south. And this fellow came here for the weekend on his way north. He was so full of the place he stayed two weeks in the end."

"I remember him," she said. "He sent me this cutting from the newspaper about Danny and the turtle he caught in the Minch—wait now; I have it here. I'll get it out if you're interested."

"I should like very much to see it," said Father James.

"A turtle in the Minch," said Father Lanni. "Most unusual—quite extraordinary, I should say." He peered at the yellow paper that was now in front of him. "Ninety pounds. My goodness! That's a great size, isn't it?"

The three men also passed the picture from hand to hand, admiring it in the dim light, and for some reason turning it over to stare at the back.

The atmosphere had warmed a little, like the first few sips of whisky on a cold night that are raw in the throat and spread out gently in the stomach afterward. Jeanie Macpherson lifted up the flap of the post office counter.

"Would you care for a cup of tea?" she said to the priests. "Come into the sitting room and m'mother'll make you one."

"Well, that's very kind of you," Father James began, "but we've just—"

"I'd be most grateful," Father Lanni said firmly. "We could do with a little refreshment."

He walked around the edge of the counter into the dark little sitting room behind, where he settled himself in the one armchair. Father James, following behind, sat on a stiff-backed chair by the window. The room faced north, like the rest of the village, and the smell of cheap soap followed them through the door as they sat and waited for their tea. Jeanie's mother came in from the kitchen and leaned against the threshold, staring at them.

"Good morning, Father Lanni," she said. "Say hello to the new father, children."

From somewhere among the folds of her apron two children dragged themselves free and ran away into the kitchen.

"They're only small," she said.

"Are those your grandchildren?" asked Father James.

"They're a fine-looking pair, Mrs. Mackay," said Father Lanni. "They're growing up fast."

"They're cunning enough, mind," she said, sighing. "It was a lovely Mass for the dead," she went on. She spoke to Father Lanni, but her eyes were fixed on the new priest.

Steam came through the door from the kitchen, and the kettle began to hiss on the range.

"I'll away and make the tea, then," she said, pushing herself off the door frame. She was back in a little while, watching the two priests sit down to their second pot of tea of the morning. The biscuits were stale and tasted of dust, but Mrs. Mackay waited in the doorway with her arms resting on her bosom until they had finished them.

"I think we must be going," said Father James, getting up. "Thank you so much for the tea."

"You're welcome."

"How is Mr. Finlay?" asked Father Lanni. The hot tea had brought out a film of damp on his forehead and upper lip. He wiped his face with a crumpled handkerchief.

"Mr. Finlay? He's the same, the very same," said Mrs. Mackay.

"And Sir John?"

"Fair getting on—he's past ninety now. And with the heat—" she shrugged and turned to the new priest. "Drop in when you like, Father. We're always here."

When he thanked her she dipped her head a little, shook

herself free of the doorpost, and went back into the kitchen. Before they were out of the sitting room door Father James could see her beyond the kitchen in her small back yard, talking to a neighbor over the fence.

Father James said good-bye to the old priest by the fork in the road and watched him drive away. The light flashed once on the roof of the car, and then it was gone into the darkness of the woods that lined the hill. Father James walked slowly along the beach. Halfway he turned around, as if he hoped to see the old Morris come back through the shadows of the trees that had swallowed it and burst out again into the sunlight of the bay. Just a little while ago he had fretted to begin on things, and now he walked idly along the edge of grass above the beach and could think of nothing whatsoever to do. The light weighed on his eyes and made them water, and the midday heat confused him.

There was a sound of someone running down the hill, jumping the dried-out ruts and spinning pebbles in the road. He looked up and saw a young girl coming toward him over the beach. She ran with her head thrown back to the sun, a great mass of red hair blowing out around her face. The skin of her arms and neck was a startling white. She was laughing, half-blinded by the light and the rushing air, half-balanced in the ancient dream that if she spread her arms she might float upward on a current of the wind. When she saw the priest she slowed down and stumbled in the road, and then she walked on primly toward him, gathering up her hair, which had shaken loose, and tying it back to the nape of her neck. She was dressed in jeans and a tight-fitting shirt, and on her feet she wore a pair of flimsy sandals that flapped as she walked along; her toes were covered with dust from the road. She might have been any age from twelve to seventeen. Father James smiled and said good morning as he passed her, but she bent her head without replying, and he heard her start to run again as he went up the hill.

He worked hard for the rest of the day. He wrote letters and prepared his weekly sermon. He studied the parish register and checked the parish supplies. And finally he read his breviary and arranged his books on the study shelves.

When he went to bed that night he felt very tired, although it was still early. He had only one clear memory of the day behind him, and the rest of his impressions were vague and confused. Before he slept he thought briefly of the girl with the dark red hair, running down the road toward the beach.

4

It was extraordinary that the housekeeper chose Saturday morning to begin one of the few conversations with Father James that she was ever to have. As soon as he sat down to breakfast, he spread out the sheets of his sermon beside him on a plate and began, for the third time that morning, to make certain he had memorized it.

"The daughters is home," Miss Morag said.

Father James sighed and put down his knife and fork. The bacon was crisp and the egg yolks a rich, creamy yellow. But Miss Morag stood over him and prevented him from enjoying them.

"The daughters?" he asked. "Whose daughters?"

"His—down the road," she said, jerking her head toward the south window.

"Mr. Finlay? But he hasn't any daughters."

"He has—two of them. Back for the holidays once a year. An aunt has them in the meantime."

"But no one's spoken to me about them."

"Not to yous they wouldn't."

Father James looked up. With one eye Miss Morag was watching him. The other eye traveled in little jumps on the wall above his head.

"What do you mean?" he asked. "I don't understand you."

"They's two beauties, Father, and you such a good-looking young priest."

She laughed and closed one eye, and the effect of this was

suddenly frightening. Father James, staring up at her from his chair, was certain for a moment that she was neither simple-minded nor insane. It was like gazing through the window of a deserted house and seeing there for a second a face staring back at him—moreover, a face that was malicious and perfectly intelligent. When she opened her other eye the feeling of horror left him, and he looked away.

"You's a nice-looking man," she said, and laughed again.

Father James rose suddenly from his chair. He was a foot and a half taller than Miss Morag. When he spoke she listened to the tones of his voice and stared without blinking at the floor.

"I think you had better go find something to do in the kitchen," he said. "I think you had better leave me to finish my breakfast in peace."

Miss Morag started toward the door, putting as much space between herself and the priest as she could manage in the narrow room. She went sideways along the edge of the table and made a scuttling rush for the door. Before she shut it behind her, she made certain that the priest had sat down again with his back to her and was eating the rest of his fried egg. She put out her tongue and drove her eyes toward the bridge of her nose in a terrible squint, and then she softly shut the door.

That same Sunday, Father James went down the road to dinner with the Finlays. As he walked up the drive and through the North Lodge gates, he heard the Kintillo River running through the thick woods to his left, faint and milky in the drought; above this, and almost drowning the sound entirely, was the noise of rooks coming home to roost in the trees above his head. Their nests hung thick and close together, and in the winter they crusted the trees like black spots where the sap had oozed out and formed ugly growths on the branches. Rhododendrons grew wild along the drive, and at their roots there was the soft bitter smell of moss and rotting undergrowth.

Half a mile along this drive the woods to one side fell away, and Father James saw the house, set deep in the middle of the valley, facing west toward the Inner Sound and the cliffs of Raasay beyond. It was cut off like an island in the center of its park, between the river on one side and the high shoulder of the hill on the other. Its isolated position gave the house a strange, sad grandeur; and because the late sun shone full on the west front, the windows were blank with light, and the place had the queer, shuttered look of a deserted building.

Father James walked up a flight of stone steps and rang the bell. While he waited he looked out across the park. The sun rested just above a rim of trees by the far sea wall, and the shadows of these trees sprang back almost the full length of the park to the edge of the gravel before the house.

A young girl let him into the hall. She wore a long wool dress, and her blond hair fell in a fine, loose sweep to her shoulders.

The hall was cold and dark. After the sunlight of the bay, he could make out nothing in that huge space but the white moonface of a grandfather clock and a number of stag's heads in rows going up the walls. He crossed the hall carefully, afraid of knocking into the umbrella stand or the rows of boots, whose shapes he could feel around him in the shadows.

The girl was waiting for him by a great mahogany door. "In here, Father," she said. "Come in."

At that moment the grandfather clock beside him struck eight, and the priest was so distracted by the noise that he tripped over a piece of the study carpet as he was going through the door. The carpet stretched from one end of the room to the other. It was so worn that the patches that dotted its surface had come unsewn; the whole effect in the late evening sun was of a roughly plowed field. It was on one of these unsewn patches that Father James now stumbled, and as he did so he knocked an ashtray from a pie-crust table onto the floor. He spent a few minutes searching for the ashtray under the sofa and rearranging it on the table, and when he straightened up, his eyes were watering with embarrassment.

The young girl asked him what he would like to drink: whisky or sherry. Gathering up her skirt and stepping neatly over the gaps in the carpet, she handed the priest a whisky and soda, then threw a log on the fire. The sparks flew up demented from its damp. In spite of the west sun that came through the windows, the air in the room was cold and a fire was burning vigorously in the grate. She picked up a silver bowl, saying, "Have some cashew nuts. Take as many as you like—there are plenty more."

The priest said, "Thank you. I'm afraid I've arrived too early."

She said not at all—that it was the maid's night off; her grandfather had taken some time getting into his wheelchair. He was heavy, and one day last summer he had fallen out of the chair onto the stone floor and broken his hip.

Father James went to the window and said, "The view from here across the sound is very beautiful."

The girl agreed; from those windows it was one of the most beautiful views on the entire west coast. She ran one hand through the thick strands of her hair and let them fall again to her neck.

She said wasn't the Aubusson carpet beautiful; it was insured for several thousand pounds—and then she blushed, remembering that Father James had tripped over it coming into the room. The priest took some cashew nuts, putting them into his mouth one by one, passing the time.

"I think I can hear my father coming now." She stood up, shaking out the folds of her skirt as though dust had gathered there.

The door opened and Charles Finlay wheeled his father into the room. The old man sat placidly with his hands folded in his lap. A tartan rug was wrapped around his knees, and his shoulders were covered with a shawl.

There are certain scenes which are impressed on the mind as if they were meant to be taken in and referred to a long time afterward. Charles Finlay seemed to search out the priest's eyes, and there was something awkward and painful about this stare which made Father James look away. His eyes were curiously dense and cold, like stones that are flawed and hold the light unevenly. They were of a remarkable blue, and there was no expression in them whatsoever.

Finlay said, "This is my father, Sir John."

He bent over the wheelchair and said distinctly, "This is the new priest, Papa: Father James."

"Father Macabe?"

"No, this is Father James. Father Macabe is dead."

The old man said nothing. One hand twitched in his lap, and he closed the palm of the other over it in a rigid grip.

"Er—Anne you've already met." Charles Finlay looked at his watch. "Meriel should be here. She's late."

The old man said loudly, "Where is Meriel—I can't see her—is she there?"

Someone spoke softly from the doorway.

"I'm here, Grandpapa."

"You're late," Finlay said. He looked at his watch again. "You're twenty minutes late."

Meriel Finlay stood in the shadows of the great mahogany door, her hand still on the doorknob, as if by letting go of it she would fall into that terrible stretch of space that separated her from the rest of them. As she crossed the floor the blood rose up in her neck and face, and the light from a lamp she passed caught the bright color of her hair. It was the same girl Father James had met, running down the road to the beach, three days before. He was so surprised that when she walked past him he said nothing, and afterward his eyes followed her with an intent expression as she settled herself on the sofa by the fire. For the minute in which he looked at her the priest was somewhere else—not in the room, nor on the beach road either, but escaped from there into some place where Meriel and the firelight and the substance of her dress were of a single beauty.

"Father," said Finlay, "do sit down." But he was standing in the way of the chairs and sofa. A moment later he asked the priest if he would like another drink. He seated himself, however, without waiting for an answer and began to study his nails attentively, lining them up in a row and examining the fine curve at the tip of each.

The priest sat down beside Anne, holding onto his empty glass because the sliver of ice at the bottom of it cooled his hands. He watched Charles Finlay take out of his pocket a thin stiletto knife—the kind that is sometimes used for opening letters. As Finlay turned the knife over and over in his hands, the light shivered up the blade. Father James began to stare at this knife, for its movement both fascinated and repelled him.

"I don't know what's happened to the dinner," Anne said. "It's only cold meat."

Her father turned slightly in his chair and looked at her. He momentarily balanced the point of the stiletto on his index finger, then caught it again with his other hand as it fell. Presently he slipped it back into his pocket and sat drumming his fingers on the arms of the chair.

When the gong rang for dinner, the four of them got up from their chairs too quickly, as if the blood had gone to sleep in their veins and needed stirring up again, and the old man was wheeled to the door and across the drafty hall.

The ancestors hung on the dining room walls in heavy frames. The silver glistened in the candlelight; the napkins were stiffly starched. Sir John sat at one end of the table and his son at the other. They were separated by twelve feet of mahogany, two great candelabra, two silver pheasants, and a silver fruit bowl.

Charles Finlay went directly to the sideboard and began to carve the cold roast beef.

Sir John leaned toward the priest, stretching his thin neck. "I'm afraid it will be cold beef," he said.

"I'm delighted," said the priest. "It will be a change from the mutton my housekeeper gives me."

The old man was no longer listening. He wiped the corners of his mouth where two patches of spittle had dried, and afterward he dropped his chin onto his chest and stared steadily in front of him. Charles Finlay sat down and his daughters passed the plates. On each plate were two slices of tender pink beef, a piece of lettuce, a tomato, and a large, feathery potato from which the butter ran out in fat gold drops.

Anne Finlay sat down beside the priest.

"Everyone knows Miss Morag is mad," she said, "but they can't find anyone to replace her."

"I must say she doesn't worry me at all," Father James said carefully. He remembered his anger that morning, and it was like a shameful secret that he shared with his housekeeper. By cutting up his beef into very small pieces and blending them with the rich paste of the butter and potato, and by resting each sip of wine against his tongue before he swallowed it, he felt the pleasure of his food rise up like sap in his body.

Charles Finlay suddenly put down his knife and fork and wiped his mouth carefully with a napkin. "You preached an odd sermon this morning," he said.

The priest cut up two more pieces of beef and put them into his mouth before replying. A vein throbbed in his neck, and he gazed at Finlay in a way which the laird's son found insolent.

"I'm afraid I don't understand," he said, "what you mean by odd."

"I thought your sermon was awfully good," Anne said. "Everyone sat up and listened to you."

"I don't think," said Finlay, ignoring her, "that your new parishioners understand you. It wasn't the kind of sermon they are accustomed to. If I were you, next Sunday I should try something a little less ambitious."

"There was nothing ambitious about it," Father James said quickly. "I simply wanted them to feel that it matters very much what they do—that the Mass should never become a routine exercise which they go through every Sunday and shut off in their minds from the rest of the week. I wanted them to feel that I'm here to give them—well, to help them to have a stronger sense of the importance of it—and the—and the purpose of it, you see—" He went on, getting more and more agitated, "For instance, when I say Mass every evening at six o'clock, no one comes. Now it's not such a great effort for some of them. I know that most people work all day, but surely a few of them could spare half an hour—I mean if they understood the importance—"

By now, however, he was aware of two things: Charles Finlay had taken his eyes off the priest's face—he was fiddling with the knives and forks around his plate, arranging them precisely in line with the table mat; Meriel, on the other hand, was gazing at him, but with a kind of intensity that seemed to have nothing to do with what he was saying. Her almond-shaped eyes were red brown, the color of her hair. Light glittered in them from the candles in front of her. The priest was so disconcerted that he immediately forgot the rest of his argument.

The meal went on in silence, which Father James no longer made an effort to break. Sir John spoke once; "I remember this theater in the Strand—St. Martin's, I think it was. I went four times to see this play by Noel Coward, but which one it was now I can't remember. . . ."

At another time, while Meriel was pouring cream on his fruit salad, he said, "And there was a restaurant on the corner of Piccadilly where I used to go before the war—Florians. I saw it one day years afterward; the sign was still there—just visible. They hadn't bombed it. . . ."

After a while he slept, his head bent over the half-empty plate and one hand curled loosely on the table beside him. Once or twice when his head reached a certain angle he woke up and stared around the table as if he had come back from a long journey. The pupils of his eyes were almost white.

When the meal was finished, Sir John was wheeled away across the hall. The worn rims of the wheelchair rang out on the bare stone hall and echoed down the back passages until the baize door finally swung shut. Anne went to make some coffee, and the priest was left alone in the study with Meriel, who bent down and threw logs on the fire, kneeling with her back to him. She swept the grate clean with a small brush and straightened the fire irons. Her hair, reaching halfway down her back, was finely waved, and there were deep bronze lights in it.

The priest sat down and cleared his throat.

"Don't you get lonely here," he said, "the whole summer on your own?"

"Oh, no," she said. "If I could, I should live here all the time. My roots are here—everything that makes me happy. But for you it's different—sent here suddenly when Father Macabe died. . . ."

"I have my work—I have a job to do."

Meriel knelt down before the fire and settled back on her heels. She started on a monologue which had just then come into her head.

"You're lucky to come here while this place is still unspoiled," she said. "When I'm in Edinburgh I have nightmares sometimes that Kintillo has changed. I dream that the Tourist Board has widened the road across the pass and filled up the beaches with caravans—that the whole bay is built over with holiday villas and car parks and refreshment rooms—"

"They won't do that for a long time. It would need an enormous amount of money, and besides, so long as there are landowners like your father—"

"But they've already begun. People are putting up bungalows in Camusrury and Camuslang with wrought iron gates and two-tone bells. And this year there were coach tours too from Fort William and Inverness."

Charles Finlay came back into the room. Without saying anything he implied that the room was untidy. He walked restlessly about for a few minutes rearranging ashtrays on the tops of tables, an inch or so one way or another. Finally he sat down and drummed his fingers again on the arms of his chair.

Anne brought in the coffee.

"Nice and strong," she said, setting down the tray.

He is definitely an army man, Father James thought, looking at Finlay. A great yawn rose up in his chest and pressed against his throat. He clenched his teeth and the yawn subsided. By stretching down to tighten a shoelace he was able to look at his watch: it was only half past nine. For the rest of the time he was there Meriel said scarcely a word. She pleated the folds of her black velvet dress in ridges between her fingers and stared dreamily at some point to the left of the fireplace. The priest had the disagreeable feeling that the whole pose was unnatural and that she was somehow forcing him to admire her profile against the light of the fire.

Finally he got up from his chair, putting down his empty coffee cup.

"I'm afraid I must go now," he said. "I have to get up very early in the morning."

Finlay considered him for a moment with his strange eyes before getting to his feet. "I'm afraid you must find it very quiet here," he said.

"Not at all—I mean, that doesn't worry me."

Charles Finlay had a strange effect on Father James. He found himself tapping the palm of one hand with the other, in the same restless manner.

"No? Good. Well, come again next Sunday. Father Macabe always came on Sunday evenings."

He walked the priest briskly to the door as if it were very late and Father James had outstayed his welcome. His daughters were already collecting the empty ashtrays and glasses as the young priest turned to say good-bye.

Charles Finlay stood for a while, watching the priest walk away down the drive into the darkness of the trees. His manner of walking alone through the stillness of the park in the coming night brought to Finlay's mind his own strange and bitter isolation; for a time it was he himself, walking in the dusk of some flat and dreary land from which there was no turning back toward the light. At that moment it seemed

to him that he would be confined to this place until such time
as he died of boredom.

So long ago now that he could remember nothing before it,
his elder brother had died, drowned at sea in a small boat
below the Summer Isles when he was twelve and Charles
only eight. The wrong brother had died: he understood this
quite clearly, and he looked after his grief alone. In the upper
reaches of the valley, he had walked by the source of the river
and watched how the water smoothed the stones, and
gradually he understood that he was like them—once jagged
and full of painful projections, but worn smooth at last and
beyond hurting, so that he no longer cared for anyone nor
anyone for him.

After his daughters said good night and shut the study
door behind them, he stayed by the window staring out into
the night, seeing nothing. A yellow square of light from the
room behind him threw his shadow across the drive and out
across the park beyond. He had been twenty-four when he
married Mary McGregor. She had sad brown eyes and
slightly dirty fingernails, but she had a languid softness too,
like a warm ripe fruit, and she had many admirers. When
Finlay married her he began immediately to worry how long
his extraordinary happiness would last. He thought of it
afterward as the warm season of his life, and it lasted until
their first child, Anne, was born. Then small changes began
to take place which he was quick to notice. Mary became
even more careless of the way she looked—her stockings often
had runs in them, and her hands, which she habitually
neglected, were rough from washing clothes and looking after
the baby. She insisted on caring for Anne herself, climbing
out of bed in the middle of the night to feed her, and letting
no one else touch her. By the time her second child was born,
her body had become thick and flabby, and the ripeness of

her breasts and hips had spread out into folds the color of putty. Besides this, she had begun to despise her husband. Her brown eyes mocked him, and from somewhere in her weak, lazy character she built up an impassive and crushing resistance to him. When he wanted to make love to her, she put down beside the bed the book she was reading, submitted without a flicker of interest, and picked up the book again as soon as he was done. She was already three months pregnant with their third child before she discussed it with him.

The baby was born too early—just three days before Mary had arranged to go home to Stirling for the birth. He was perfectly made, with long delicate hands and thick dark hair, but he lived for only an hour, and two days later his mother died of a massive hemorrhage. Finlay mourned her death in several ways; he protested against her total absence, he bemoaned the monstrous perfection of his son, and finally he grieved for the love that he had lost so many years before. And all these things were like the separate sources of some great flood which was draining steadily out of him and leaving him wasted and empty again.

Mary's sister had taken charge of his daughters, taking them to Edinburgh with her. They lived there until they were old enough to look after themselves; then they spent their summer holidays in Kintillo. And it was at this thought that Finlay, standing by the open curtains with a draft coming up from the loose-fitting window ledge, became agitated, going over and over the same ground. He knew that something was wrong, yet he was unable to find a way of putting it right. His daughters were the only two things in his life that he had actually achieved; they were his blood, incredible seeds from his own body, and yet they seemed to have nothing to do with him. Anne looked so much like him that at times he seemed to be staring into his own eyes and seeing a vacuum there. Perhaps he gave them too little—or, on the other hand, too much: every year he had their bedrooms repainted in colors they chose, he bought them good horses to ride, he wrote to each of them once a week, sometimes twice; was this enough? He had no way of knowing, no one to tell him anything. And then there was the new priest, with that fresh, timid smile. . . . Charles Finlay clenched one hand and rapped it without thinking against the cold windowpane. To come into the study after dinner and find them chattering there together, he on the sofa and Meriel at his feet, to watch the interest leave their faces, when he walked in as if he were a stranger. Nevertheless, it was out of the question to put the priest off—it was necessary to submit week after week now, for God knew how long, to these Sunday evenings, to Father James's intolerable enthusiasm and charm.

In spite of his indignation, Finlay plumped up the cushions in each chair before he went to bed, placed the fireguard in front of the dead fire, and emptied the last cigarette butts into its ashes.

That night, when the priest slept, he had a series of feverish dreams. In one of them Sir John was walking down the beach with two little girls. The sun was hot and the sea was a dark, warm blue. The children were pulling on his arms to make him run, and behind them, stuck fast in the damp sand, Charles Finlay sat in a wheelchair. The sound of his furious shouting was carried away on the wind. One child, when she looked up, had eyes of a light red-brown.

5

The next morning when Meriel came down to breakfast Anne was sitting alone at the table, reading the newspapers. She seemed absorbed by the headlines and neither looked up from the paper nor said good morning. Meriel shrugged and began to lift the silver covers off the dishes on the sideboard. One by one she lifted them, savoring the smell of the food in each. In the first there was porridge, in the second a fine kipper, and in the third some fried eggs and bacon. The eggs were cooked just the way she liked them—the whites crisp and the yolks a pale, dense yellow.

"Well," Anne said suddenly, "you sat around all evening like a dummy and left me to do all the talking."

"What?" said Meriel. She lifted the fried eggs tenderly onto a plate and poured herself a cup of coffee.

"I was talking about last night."

"Ah, last night. . . ."

Meriel sat down. She gazed out of the window for a minute before beginning her breakfast. It was a perfect summer day. The shadows of the trees across the park had begun to fill out in the morning sun. Beyond them she could just make out the thin line of Raasay, rising from the sea.

"The priest," Anne was saying, "had a remarkable kind of beauty." He reminded her of certain statues, broken-nosed though they were, that she had seen in the Adam Museum in Edinburgh.

Meriel put down her knife and fork and began to laugh.

"No, wait," she said as Anne got up. "I'm sorry—I didn't meant to laugh at you. To tell the truth, I had forgotten about the priest. I couldn't even tell you what he looks like now."

It was true: until that minute she had scarcely thought about the new priest.

When she was totally self-absorbed, Meriel very often failed to take in what was straight in front of her. Sometimes she looked at certain people second-hand: if, for instance, her sister made some comment on them, she would immediately alter her own vague impressions and adapt them to this new image. There was no denying, now that she thought about it, that Father James was a good-looking man.

She took a piece of toast, spread it thickly with butter and marmalade, and ate it greedily. Anne was gazing at her with her hands on her hips.

"I don't understand you," she said. "I don't understand you at all. Anyone who comes to dinner in this place is a big event. Father James is probably the only new face we shall see this side of the autumn, and you can't even remember what he looks like."

Meriel smiled up at her.

"I can't help it," she said. "He made no impression on me. He had yellow hair and blue eyes. As for the rest—he was quiet, almost timid. He hardly spoke, did he?"

She was irritating her sister and she knew it. She began to hum a little tune which had just then come into her head as she stretched across the table for the newspaper.

Anne stopped by the door on her way out.

"When you are in this kind of mood," she said, "there is no point in talking to you."

"What kind of mood?"

"If Papa needs me for anything, tell him I shall be out on the drive practicing my three-point turns."

When she had gone, Meriel poured herself a second cup of coffee and sat down again at the table. She was in an excellent mood. She felt healthy and contented. There had been a time, not long ago, when she was able to count up the number of her conquests on the fingers of one hand. And then in the course of the last summer all this had changed. In the same way as a fully opened flower will suddenly attract bees from all the neighboring bushes, so Meriel, who to her own way of thinking had scarcely changed, found herself with a great number of new admirers.

She put three lumps of sugar into her coffee and stirred it slowly. In some way that she could not name, the summer had turned out to be strangely lonely. A cold rain had fallen day after day, and the Edinburgh streets were bleak and slippery, with a fine black dust from the coal fields in Midlothian. And Meriel, when she thought of the number of men who had kissed her, could only remember them now in connection with the steady sound of falling rain. One night she had also lost her virginity, and this, like other new experiences before it, had turned out to be a bewildering and uncomfortable affair. In the morning her lover had dressed without once looking her in the face and had left by the basement door without kissing her good-bye. Now, when she considered this time as a whole and from a distance, a sudden impatience filled her; she got up from the table quickly without bothering to finish her coffee and went out into the sunlight.

She leaned against one of the stone balustrades that led down either side of the great front steps and raised her face to the warmth of the sun. She began to sing to herself the first song that came into her head. Below her the moving grass, the dark summer trees, and even the sheep grazing in the shade seemed to her like the parts of a single picture especially designed to please her. But presently this impression was entirely ruined by the sound of Anne coming up the drive in the Land-Rover.

Neither of the two sisters had passed their driving tests, and this failure obsessed Anne to the point where she would practice reversing and emergency stops again and again on the drive in front of the house. But while Anne confined herself to the roads around the park, and took care not to ruin the gearbox, Meriel drove fast and carelessly along every road in the peninsula. Last year she had run over a sheep by Camusrury. The sheep had a broken leg and one of the shepherds had been forced to shoot it.

Anne drove past the front steps twice, changing gears smoothly and looking at the same time, for some reason, in the mirror. The third time she went past her, Meriel shouted, "Hey—how long will you be?"

Anne turned the Land-Rover neatly along the grass verge and came to a stop. She leaned out of the window.

"I wish you wouldn't stand there staring at me," she shouted back. "You make me nervous."

Meriel came down the steps at a leisurely pace and wandered across the gravel. She had fine long legs and she walked in a lazy, graceful way that indicated that she was entirely conscious of them.

"I'm going to see Magnus," she said. "When you've finished with the Land-Rover I'll take it."

Anne looked at her watch.

"I'll be at least another half hour—you can have if after that—though what you see in that old drunkard," she added, "I shall never know."

Meriel closed her eyes and smiled.

"Well, he's like a second father to me now," she said gently.

Magnus Laver was sitting on a bench outside his cottage door. It occurred to him to go in and boil up a kettle for some tea, and then almost immediately he decided against it. It was warm in the sun, and the inside of his cottage was cold and damp.

The sun was like a benediction, day after day of it, such weather as he had never seen in the entire ten years he had lived in the Toscaig cottage.

Magnus had once been a London doctor. But about the same time as his teeth had fallen out, the result of a gum infection, he had begun to drink too much and to take an interest in philosophy. Over the next few years he continued to practice medicine, but during this time a great gap was springing up between the suffering of his patients and his ability to cure them. The chronically sick still died, the middle-aged still complained, and in the middle of their inevitable paths the doctor with his bag of medicines stood confused, the whisky sometimes in his brain.

Throughout this time, he had a certain longing, a dream that he had never actually dreamed, or a picture that he might have seen without remembering where, of a clouded wild coastline where the sea was a constant line of spray against the rocks and where the mountain peaks were cut off from month to month by a thick mist. It was a place he had never been in the whole of his life. The dream continued to haunt him, and one day Magnus gave in to it: he decided at last to give up his practice. He put up his small London flat for sale and six months later climbed into his car with his books and luggage and drove north. There was a Doctor Roberts who regularly sent him Christmas cards, a man he had met once at a medical conference, who lived in Ballahuilish. Magnus liked the name of the place; it was on his way, and he drove northwest toward it. As he was driving along he spoke to his wife, Mary, who had been dead for several years.

"It's strange," he said. "Mary, when you died I hardly touched a drink—and yet, when they took my teeth away, I gave in like a baby after the teat."

Later he sang, to keep his mind off the pubs that were opening up along the road.

When he reached Ballahuilish, his friend, the local doctor, exchanged glances with his wife while Magnus was out of the room, unpacking. It's a pity, these glances indicated, that Doctor Laver has let himself go to such an extent.

"I saw an advertisement for this house in Applecross," Magnus said after the evening meal.

"Beautiful," the doctor agreed, again looking quickly at his wife. "A little remote, but it will do no harm to go and look at it."

"I've already leased it," Magnus said, grinning. A moment later he lit a small cigar. "I was annoyed by my solicitors—I found them too cautious, you see, and when they advised me against it, I decided to lease the place."

"And you've never even seen it?"

This time the local doctor and his wife avoided each other's eyes and stared at the floor between them. Magnus removed his false teeth and tucked them into the breast pocket of his coat. He smiled at his hostess.

"I have trouble with these teeth," he said. "In general, I wear them only when I play the clarinet, for otherwise the tone would be affected."

Mrs. Roberts fiddled with a strand of hair that had escaped from the fine net she wore over it.

"It's been a pleasure meeting you again, Doctor," she said, "but if you'll excuse me, I'll away to my bed now."

Doctor Roberts put the fireguard firmly down in front of

the fire. "I'm sure you'll have a fine cottage, Doctor Laver," he said. "A fine bargain."

Magnus took the Ballahuilish ferry next morning across Loch Leven, with a picnic lunch prepared by Mrs. Roberts and a bottle of Drambuie that he bought later in Fort William. When he reached the pass of Tornapress, which separated Kintillo from the mainland behind it, Magnus climbed out of his car and looked up at the great black horseshoe ridge with its back to the sun. The road ahead was very narrow—a thin strip that crawled steeply up the mountain shoulder—and around each bend was the sense that it would fall away altogether on the other side. When he climbed back into his car, there was a dark rim around his field of vision from staring into the shadows, and his hands trembled on the steering wheel, for he was mortally afraid of heights. On the ferry, the doctor had taken a few mouthfuls of Drambuie straight from the bottle, which now lay beside him on the seat, rolling backward and forward with the tilt of each corner.

"If I can just keep my hands off it until I reach the top," said Magnus, "we shall be all right."

His knees began to shake and his breath came in short gasps, as though he were running up the heights instead of driving them. Behind him and to the side the pass fell away into a mighty trough, and beyond that, strangely, the sun was out. It was shining on loch Hourn, three thousand feet below.

"God help me," said Magnus when he reached the top. "This is far enough away for anyone." He sighed and uncorked the bottle of Drambuie.

The Toscaig cottage came as a shock to him, for it had never been included in his dreams. There was a thin, sad light on the winter hills, and the place looked derelict. A mountain ash grew deep into the walls on one side. The windows were lopsided and crooked in their frames.

"Don't you think," Magnus said to the laird's factor, who stood beside him, "it's a bit ramshackle for the price?"

The factor too had been astonished by the rent. He lowered his eyes and fiddled with the keys in his trouser pocket.

"You'd be best to take it, however," he said, "if you've a mind to live here. The laird has only three or four cottages to let, and the others are already taken. You could go back," he said, still gazing at the ground, "to Fort William and try there for somewhere else. I doubt if you'll find so much, though."

"I have already signed the lease," Magnus said. "And besides, there is the godforsaken pass—I haven't the stomach to cross it twice in one day. . . .

"It'll do," he said at last. He turned and went back down the hill to fetch his luggage.

Magnus had lived in the Toscaig cottage now for more than ten years. It had no electricity and no bathroom. The roof leaked intermittently, and when it rained he would feel an ache in his kneecaps and in the joints of his fingers. He was entrenched there, however. He was too old and too weary to go south again.

Suddenly he sat up stiffly and rubbed his eyes. Someone was singing, coming up the hill, out of sight on the steep slope below him. Sighing, Magnus got slowly to his feet.

When he saw Meriel Finlay a few yards below him on the path, he took his false teeth from his pocket and put them back into his mouth. Meriel stopped for a moment on the edge of the hill to catch her breath, and the doctor hurried forward to kiss her on both cheeks. He led her toward the bench, which he dusted with a crumpled handkerchief and pulled out a little from the wall.

"Ah, it's good to see you," he said. "It's good to see your beautiful face."

Meriel sat down on the bench beside him and smiled at him. "Well," she said presently, "I like to come up here and listen to your Irish compliments."

Magnus burst out laughing. "And you," he said, patting her hand, "—you get prettier every time I see you."

Meriel leaned back against the cottage wall and shielded her eyes from the light. Below them across the Inner Sound the tip of Raasay sloped down into the sea, and beyond Raasay the mountains of Skye rose clear from the narrow straits between; their peaks blue in the morning sun.

"You have the best view, Magnus, in the whole of Kintillo."

"So I have," he agreed. "I pay for it, however. I pay a handsome rent for it."

He had forgotten to eat any breakfast. His stomach felt like an empty pit, and from time to time the walls of this pit swelled in and out in gentle spasms.

"I came up to see you before I go," Meriel was saying. "Anne and I have been asked to stay for a week with cousins in Portree."

"Ah. . . ."

"I shan't enjoy it, though. The cousins feel sorry for us. They wonder what we do all day cooped up here with no parties to go to."

Magnus studied her. He clicked his teeth together.

"Well," he said. "What do you do here—what is there for a girl of your age to do here?"

Meriel shrugged. "I'm naturally lazy," she answered. "I can sit around for hours at a time and do nothing."

"Nothing at all?" Magnus seemed incredulous.

"Well, I suppose I dream a lot." For some reason she

blushed and avoided looking at the doctor's face. "I mean, it passes the time."

Magnus straightened up on the bench. "It seems peculiar to me," he started, "that at your age, when you have almost no memories worth dreaming of, nothing in fact in the way of experience—"

In the middle of this sentence his stomach rumbled loudly and Meriel began to laugh. "You haven't eaten your breakfast yet, have you?"

"It's true, I could do with a cup of tea," he said apologetically. "I tell you what—you could put on a kettle now for us both."

While she was inside the cottage, the doctor leaned back against the wall and stretched out his legs in front of him.

"What a day," he said sighing. "Ah, what a day." The sun was coming down in a slant across the bay, and the air was full of a light south wind that carried a smell of bracken and fresh thyme along the shoulder of the hill.

Meriel came back a few minutes later. "There's no paraffin for the stove," she said, "and the fire has gone out too."

"Ah, has it indeed." He thought for a moment. "Then you could bring us some glasses and the whisky that you will find sitting there by the sink—it's near midday, after all," he added.

Presently she came back with the bottle and two glasses and set them down on the ground.

"All the glasses are chipped," she said, smiling at him, "and the time by my watch is only half past ten."

Magnus giggled guiltily, and while he was pouring out the drinks, he spilled a little whisky on the grass.

"Aah," said Meriel. The alcohol burned her throat and brought tears to her eyes. She sipped at it a little at a time, gazing at the color in the liquid's reflection.

"I like it here," she said comfortably. "This is a place where I can talk. I can tell you almost anything."

They talked for almost two hours. Meriel leaned forward from time to time and picked up a few pebbles from the ground. She examined them briefly, tossed them around between her hands, and threw them down again. In the same erratic way, the two of them discussed whatever came into their heads, lightly and without following any one train of thought. Suddenly Meriel looked at her watch and jumped up from the bench.

"Look at the time," she said. "It's five to one."

"Ah, relax now," said Magnus. He was no longer hungry. The whisky had restored his vitality. "Relax for another five minutes, why don't you? You have the Land-Rover down there."

Meriel shook her head. "No—I really have to go. My father is an army man. He hates unpunctuality." She kissed him good-bye and stood looking at him for a moment before starting down the path. "What did you look like," she said smiling, "with your real teeth? I can't imagine you."

"One day I will find you a photograph of myself as a young man," he promised her. "I was really handsome then. My wife Mary chased after me until I married her."

He walked with her a little way down the path and waited afterward until the Land-Rover had disappeared around a corner of the road.

Presently he found a tin of sardines in a cupboard by the sink, and he ate them straight from the tin, with a book propped up beside him on the bench outside.

6

In the small villages of the Peninsula, the same things happen over and over again. Even the unexpected has a double image to it, as if it had occurred sometime before in the same way and in the same place. There is a pattern to the week—the mailboat on Saturday, Mass on Sunday, the weekly wash on Monday—and so the memory shortens itself and goes from day to day. The pattern is lost among the individual threads, and you could be very busy just passing the time in the village shop, or prodding about with a stick on the forestry commission land.

In the same way, without noticing it, Father James's ambitions began to shrink to the size of the place he lived in. He gave up hoping for a choir that would do more than sing the carols on Christmas day. He inquired about an organ for the church, but he gave this up too, because the roof still needed mending, and when the autumn rains came it would leak again over the altar rails.

He decided, however, to tackle the paintwork inside the rectory. But events had a habit of slipping away and being put off for the future. Mactaggart the village painter had recently died. Father James himself had closed the dead man's eyelids and given him extreme unction, and it was Rory Mactaggart the younger who came up to the rectory one morning and moved all the furniture out of the study into the narrow hall.

He said, "Father, would you like a decent job with the

blowlamp? Some of this paint's been on the woodwork for over a hundred years."

It was safe to reckon that the diocese would pay for this. "Yes, indeed," the priest said. "I think that's an excellent idea."

"And then there's this new paint against the damp," Mactaggart said. "You'd be as well to have that—it's expensive, mind, but it's worth it."

"Yes—well, that sounds all right."

"Now, you can have a third-rate job done, Father—what you would call an economic patching-up schedule on the one hand—"

"No, I would rather—"

"—or you can have a first-rate job, on the other hand, which will last you the time you're here—"

"Yes, I think. . . ."

"—and well after. This place is in a shocking state, as you can see."

Miss Morag was in the hall behind them. Father James felt the small hairs at the back of his neck rise up in the draft through the kitchen door.

"Well, I'll leave it to you," he said, "to do the first-class job, er—Mr. Mactaggart."

"Rory, Father—I'm always Rory to the patrons."

"Rory, then—just as long as you do it as quickly as you can."

"Certainly, Father, certainly. If Miss Morag could just fix me up with a cup of tea now, I'll start on it first thing tomorrow morning."

"Tomorrow?" the priest said. "But I thought you were starting right away."

"Ah, well—but I've the van to bring up—the materials and so forth I shall be needing for the duration. And then there's the job I was on when you rang me, Father, down at

Thompson's Farm. Naturally I dropped everything to come up here and see you."

"Well, I'm very grateful—but I thought you said on the telephone you could start straightaway. Right in on it, you said."

Miss Morag was polishing the same strip of bannister she had been polishing for half an hour now. The priest turned sharply.

"Will you get Mr. Mactaggart a cup of tea, please," he said. While she was going out through the door he noticed that his hands were tightly clenched.

"I'll be up first thing in the morning, Father," Mactaggart said, putting his cap back on his head. "About nine—will that suit you?"

"Yes, that'll be fine," the priest said. As Rory was halfway through the door to the kitchen he said quickly:

"Perhaps you could come to Mass, Rory, first—at half past eight."

"Er, no, thank you, Father—I'm a Protestant."

"A Protestant? I'm sorry—I thought I saw your name on the parish register."

"Er, well—I'm a Protestant convert, you see. About nine tomorrow then. I'll make a grand job of it."

Rory Mactaggart turned up the next day, but his blowlamp was temperamental, and Father James understood that he himself would do without his study for some time and would go on grazing his shin on the furniture in the narrow hall almost every time he went up and down the stairs.

One midday the priest was lying outside the rectory in the long grass, reading his breviary. Once this grass had been a lawn, but now it was tangled and spotted with dark patches of clover and sea flowers that resisted the salt west wind, and it was hemmed in by a tumbled wall from which about a quarter of the stones had fallen down on either side. Now the

wall stood rickety and stump-toothed and the grass grew up
its sides almost to the top. The grass was cool and sweet-
smelling of shriveled pinks and wild thyme and lemon balm.
He crushed the lemon balm between his fingers because this
scent reminded him of a summer long ago when, lying in a
field looking up through the thick grass stems, he saw a whole
new country there, two inches from the ground.

"I had an early meal," said Rory Mactaggart. He leaned
through the window with the unlit blowlamp in one hand.
He held the blowlamp like a tankard cradled against his
chest. The priest put down his breviary and straightened up
on one elbow in the grass.

"It's grand weather we're having," said Mactaggart.

The priest agreed. The shadows of the sycamores shifted
up and down and the grass moved a little in a lift of wind.

"I hear you're thinking of having a jumble sale, Father."

The priest sat upright. "I was only discussing it an hour
ago in the village shop," he said. "I'm amazed—" he
stopped.

"Things travel," Mactaggart said. "You might say the
very stones are listening in."

"It's only an idea so far," the priest said, "and it won't
make much money this year or even next. But the main point
is not the money we'll get out of it—" He turned and looked
up toward the point where Rory Mactaggart was leaning on
the windowsill.

"It's the chance to get the parish together, to get them
working on something outside themselves, all those people
who have nothing to do, who are isolated or lonely or
neglected in some way."

Mactaggart scratched one ear with the handle of the
blowlamp.

"Excuse me, Father," he said, "but you're not talking

about anybody I know. Everyone has something to do, even if it's just sitting on the doorstep smoking a pipe—"

"But how many of you really work? I mean a good day's work, with wages in your pockets to spend?"

"Well," Mactaggart said, "I should say about half the population. So long as the laird is alive and his son after him."

"Only half. Well then, you see? It's ridiculous. At least I could find work for some of you—not permanent perhaps, but there are plenty of things to be done that badly need doing."

"Excuse me, Father, but what things?"

"Well, according to Father Lanni—"

"With respect to your profession, Father, he's a fool. He's a fool who has lived here for decades and understands nothing about the place at all. He says, 'Get the Forestry Commission up here—plant fir trees—forests of firs.' Would you like to see these hills covered in dark green squares and triangles? Regular regiments of them? And who would get the real benefit? Not us, not the people who live here. He says, 'Get the fishing industry going.' He knows nothing about it. Does he know, for instance, that the lobster fishers are going as far south as Northumberland to find work? That they tip the fish back into the sea for lack of transport? That right this year they've closed the railway to Inverness from the Kyle and they're even talking now of closing the tracks to Mallaig, the biggest fishing port on this part of the coast? He knows nothing."

"And yet," the priest said, getting to his feet, then sitting down again, propped against the garden wall, "and yet he is right about one thing. With the present rate of people leaving this coast, in twenty years' time there will be no one living here. Unless something is done to hold them back, in fifty years the roads will go to ruin and this area will be uninhabitable. I've wanted to come here for a long time. I've read all I could find about the place—your history, your economy, your traditions. Unless you fight for them now, and quickly, they'll be gone during your lifetime."

"That's been said from a long way back," Mactaggart said mildly. He put the blowlamp down on the windowsill and gazed out across the bay. "It was said at the rising of the '45. It was said in the Year of the Sheep and about every year since."

"That doesn't mean it won't finally happen."

Mactaggart shrugged. "Why did you want to come up here, Father?"

Suddenly the priest flushed. "I don't think I could answer that in a way you would understand. And besides, I don't see what that has to do with anything we were saying." He stopped to brush the grass seed from his black cloth suit. Across the beach the children let out of school ran zigzag up and down the sand, throwing stones at the sea gulls, and the sea gulls were screaming from the water's edge as if they had actually been hit.

"Then if I had to guess," the painter said, "I'd say suppose you came here to get away—to get away from all those troubles in the south, from the dirty air to this air that's sweet and clean, from all that chasing after money to this place where there's not much money and nothing to spend it on. Suppose you came here because—"

"I didn't come here to get away. I came here to do something."

"Suppose you came here because we've a different kind of trouble here—something a man could get hold of and change. Maybe you can't change the other because it's going too fast. One man can't do much in a big city—just a little here and there. But in this place he would have a chance to breathe and to make something of himself and the place he lives in. No offense meant, Father, but there are plenty others of you out there along this coast."

"Others of me?" The priest was getting restless. His lunch was late. But an odd politeness kept him there when he should have gone back into the house.

"Don't you see, Father," Mactaggart said patiently, "so long as there's others of you longing for the empty land—and there's plenty of them—so long as there's others coming here to get away from the big cities, and so long as there's some of us content to live here too, the way we've always done, then the Highlands will survive. And that," he said, "will be anyways until I die."

Miss Morag was at the rectory door, pulling and kicking at the bottom where it had dropped on its hinges with the damp.

"I'm coming," the priest shouted.

Rory Mactaggart put his head back through the window and lit the blowlamp.

"Your dinner's on the table," Miss Morag said. She had finally opened the door and was standing there shielding her face from the brilliant sun.

As the priest walked into the dining room Mactaggart appeared again, this time around the study door.

"Excuse me, Father," he said. "But about the jumble sale—no sense in hurrying things."

Before the priest had his mouth open to reply, Mactaggart's head had disappeared again around the door and he began to sing above the tearing of the blowlamp.

Something happened in the following week that put the jumble sale entirely out of Father James's mind.

He came back very late from Dornie on Sunday night, and the following morning he went into the post office to collect his groceries.

"Did you not hear, Father?" the postmistress said in her calm voice. "Rory Mactaggart broke three ribs and both his legs last Saturday after the football match in Glasgow. He fell from a window thirty feet—it's a miracle he's still alive."

The priest was astonished. "What a terrible thing," he said. "How did it happen?"

"Well, he had this fight in a bar on Sauchiehall Street—a fight with a rival football fan. His ear was sliced off by a bottle—and seeing how much he had drunk, he felt no pain. Well," she went on, "when he saw the kind of hospital they had taken him to, poor Rory forgot about the stairs and took a dive from the first-floor window to get out of it again."

"I'm really sorry to hear that—what a terrible thing," he said again.

"And then the ear," she added. "I think they found it afterward in the road. Is there anything else you'll be needing then, Father?"

As the priest drove home, his astonishment grew. Rory was a gentle man not connected in his mind with football matches and violent accidents, nor indeed with the big cities which he seemed to despise. These events appeared to have happened to a different man, one he had never met.

When he reached the rectory, he put the heavy box of groceries down on the kitchen table. Miss Morag was standing as she always did pressed into the darkest shadows in a corner of the room.

"There's a young lady to see you."

"A young lady? Who?"

"Miss Meriel—she's in the church. She wants confession."

"Oh," said the priest. He turned away and looked out of the window as though he expected to see her standing there inside the vestry door. He could just make out the church through the heavy dark leaves of the sycamore trees. The idea of hearing Meriel Finlay's confession was somehow disagreeable to him.

"I won't be long," he said. "I'll have my lunch at the usual time."

Inside the vestry there was no sound at all—nothing, in fact, to indicate that Meriel Finlay was there behind the screen. The air in the small room was stifling. The pine chair creaked as he sat down in it.

Meriel cleared her throat. "It's three weeks since my last confession," she began.

Father James gazed out of the vestry window. The sky was a single square of plain blue and half another. The sun was a long way above him on the gray slate roof. As Meriel went through her minor faults, the priest said nothing. He waited to see what had brought her up the hill on such a beautiful weekday morning.

She told him, at last, that there was nothing to do in Kintillo—the weather was hot, and she would sit sometimes on the beach alone and long for someone to make love to her. And again in bed at night the same thoughts would go on tormenting her until she was sick of them and could not sleep.

At times she spoke so softly that the priest had to lean against the screen to hear her at all. "How old are you?" he asked her presently.

"Nineteen."

"Well then, at your age these thoughts are perfectly normal. It's only when they become an obsession or even a habit that there is anything wrong in them."

"But I am obsessed—"

At this point he was suddenly incredulous. He felt certain, without knowing why, that her entire confession was false.

"Are you obsessed?" he asked gently.

There was no answer from behind the screen. Father James sighed. He tilted the chair back slightly and stretched his legs, for they had been pressed against the wall in one position.

"I don't ask you to suppress these thoughts entirely," he said in a flat monotone. "I would like you, however, to try to control them a little. And, if it's possible, to spend less time on your own. It is wrong for a girl of your age to be alone too much."

In general, the confessions he was hearing would sift through his mind without leaving a single impression. Very often they were simply a list repeated from one confession to the next, so that, like a doctor listening again and again to the same complaints, he would give out the same penances and repeat the same small homilies.

Sometimes he was moved by pity or even sympathy; at other times, however, he would feel a sudden sharp impatience. There was, for instance, a small group of people, mostly frustrated married women or young girls, who would deliberately set out to shock him. They would describe their married lives to him in great detail, leaving nothing out, or they would lean against the screen and try to provoke him into discussions on sex and morality. It had occurred to him, while he was listening to Meriel Finlay, that she might be one of these. Then almost immediately he was ashamed of himself.

He asked her if she had anything else to confess. She told him there was nothing—nothing of any importance.

"Then make a good act of contrition and pray to God to give you peace of mind."

A wasp was trapped against the vestry window. The window was open (in fact, it was warped and would not shut), but the wasp repeatedly climbed up the bottom pane as far as the wooden surround, then fell to the ledge, then started out again on the same journey a second later. This noise distracted the priest and interfered with the words of absolution.

"In the name of the Father," he said, raising his voice, "and of the Son, and of the Holy Ghost."

"Amen."

"Go in peace," he said as Meriel got up to leave, "and pray for me."

When he came out of the church she was standing awkwardly in the middle of the cinder path waiting for him. She wore a gray pleated skirt, dark nylon stockings and a black blazer, and Father James was even more irritated, seeing that she had dressed up specially for the occasion.

"I'm sorry," she said, "but my father told me to tell you, if I saw you again soon, that perhaps you could come to dinner every other Sunday—my grandfather's getting too old now, you see. . . ."

He nodded. "Tell him I'll come once a month instead— perhaps that's better. Tell him I'll ring him."

"All right, I'll tell him that." She started off down the cinder path at once. The priest turned away and went back through the rectory gate. As he shut it behind him, he couldn't avoid seeing, from a distance, the deep copper red of Meriel's hair as she went down the road. She was running again, like a child let out of school.

7

Meriel could no more stop herself from running down that hill than the birds on the beach below her could stop from rising, singly or in thick flocks, circling for a time in the warmth of the sun, and settling again in the same patches of sand as before. And so long as she was running, she had no worries at all, felt nothing but the wind lifting her hair and the heat of the midday sun in her face.

But when she reached the foot of the hill, she was out of breath and sat down for a while on the bridge. This bridge crossed the mouth of the Kintillo River. On one side the water was clear and ran freely, but on the other it sank almost without a trace into the silt of the bay. Meriel leaned against the bridge and looked down into the water, and then abruptly, as though she had seen her own reflection there, she got up and began to walk on along the road.

She was mortally ashamed of herself. No one in the whole of Kintillo had ever seen her in a skirt; and even worse than this, she was parading along the beach at midday in high-heeled shoes and dark stockings. She turned quickly through the lodge gates into the shade of the north drive. Here she was hidden from the park by a thick belt of trees and from the open valley by the side woods. The side woods were cold and secretive. As a child it had seemed to her that a person might die there and that his body would be overgrown with creepers and one day resemble nothing but a fallen log to anyone passing by. Just then, however, she found the darkness comforting, and presently she slowed down and began to walk again in her usual slouching way. She considered the morning behind her with a mixture of shame and fear.

That morning, as usual, she had dressed hurriedly and without interest, picking up a pair of jeans from the floor where she had thrown them down the night before. As she zipped them up, she could see through the window her sister on a bay mare, trotting down the drive toward the road. Anne wore smart gray breeches and her hair was tied in a bun. As she rose up and down to the movement of the trot, the seat of her breeches caught the light, and presently Meriel, watching her from the window, began to imitate her, sticking out her bottom and rising up and down in the same precise and finicky manner. In the middle of this charade, however, she stopped what she was doing and stood with her arms hanging loose at her sides, for she had seen her own reflection in the dressing table mirror. She was still naked to the waist, and in the strong light from the window her body looked magnificent. The flesh of her arms and neck was white and smooth, and beneath her breasts there were two deep shadows the shape of crescent moons. She stood there for a moment longer, turning slightly from one side to the other so that the light caught her body from different angles, and then she sat down to brush her hair.

From time to time in the past week Meriel had allowed her thoughts to rest lightly on the priest. She had made up a number of daydreams about him, and at first these were almost harmless. But now while she sat half-naked on the dressing stool she smiled at her reflection in the mirror. This smile was sly and secretive, for an amazing scene had just then come into her head. There were only two figures in this scene, and one of them was Father James. He was standing at the rectory door in the morning sun, and before him, wearing a light fawn raincoat and flimsy sandals, stood Meriel Louisa Finlay.

"Come in," the priest was saying. He stood a little back from the door. "What can I do for you?"

Meriel walked ahead of him into the small study. Her eyes were cast down, and she stood in the middle of the room with her hands clasped neatly in front of her.

"I'm afraid it's a little stuffy in here." The priest made an effort to open the window, but the runners were loose, and almost immediately it closed again. "Do sit down, won't you," he said, turning around, "and take off your things."

"Thank you, Father."

Obediently his guest began to take off her coat. With one hand she undid the buttons, and with the other she modestly held the edges shut. When the last button was undone, she stepped out of it neatly and allowed it to fall to the floor. Beneath the raincoat Meriel had on nothing at all.

At this point in her daydream Meriel covered her mouth with her hands and started to laugh. And when she looked in the mirror her eyes were shining brilliantly.

"One day," she said softly to herself aloud, "I will do it."

She picked up the hairbrush again and tilted her head backward so that the whole tender weight of her hair fell down her back almost to the waist. Just as she longed to go up the hill dressed in such a way, she could see at once that she would do nothing of the kind. The rest of this little scene was not clear to her at all, and besides, it was certain to turn out badly.

Presently another plan began to form in her mind—one that was altogether different and almost harmless. She settled herself more comfortably on the stool and began to make up her eyes. She spread two wings of shadow across each lid and applied a thick coat of mascara to the upper and lower lashes. Presently she searched out, among the muddle in her drawers, her last good pair of stockings, her cleanest shirt, and a smart pleated skirt.

In the same excellent spirits she walked up the road to the rectory and knocked on the door, and while she stood there waiting for the priest, she briefly revised the confession she had just made up.

There were two things wrong with her plan, however, which she had not foreseen. From the beginning of her confession Meriel had felt a sense of shame, and this feeling reached a point where she longed to get up and leave again. And later, while she stood talking with the priest on the cinder path outside, something totally unexpected and painful had taken place. For Meriel, looking up for a minute into the priest's face, had seen in his eyes her own reflection, and this reflection seemed immediately cheap and repulsive to her.

She had now walked the entire length of the north drive without noticing her surroundings. Within a hundred yards of the house the thick trees fell away to either side of it, and the broad light of the midday sun cut into the edges of the woods. The house looked white and shrunken in the glare, and the open park was deserted.

Meriel calculated that it would take her about half a minute to reach the side door and another to get to the safety of her room. With her shoes in one hand, she ran in her stocking feet across the gravel. She reached the side door just as the gun dogs began to bark in the stable yard. The stone back stairs were cold underfoot, and she stumbled in the unaccustomed darkness. No sound came up the stairwell from the kitchen, and the first-floor landings were empty. Most of the bedrooms had been cleaned and the windows and doors left open so that a fresh cool draft ran through the upper hall and along the usually airless passages.

Meriel shut her bedroom door and leaned against it

resting. She took off the pleated skirt and left it lying on the floor. She threw down the blazer in the same way. Then she lit a cigarette and surveyed the room. There were piles of unfolded clothes on a chair and on the floor around the bed. On her dressing table were jars without tops and an empty Kleenex box stuffed with rubbish. From time to time Meriel would sort out the bottles and jars and hang up the clothes in the closet again. But generally these fits of tidiness would begin to seem pointless after a short while, and the mess would then build up again gradually and without being noticed.

That morning, however, the whole room disgusted her, and she started to work on it with a sudden impatience. She cleared the floor, the dressing table, and even the insides of the drawers. And by the time the gong rang for lunch she was hot from the unaccustomed work and quite satisfied with the general effect. The bed was neatly made and the cover drawn over it. Fresh air had lifted the smell of cigarettes from the room, and the full south sun shone at an angle across the empty floor.

But in the evening of that same day, for no reason at all, a bewildering sadness filled her. For a long while she sat looking out of the window, gazing at nothing, and later she wrote in the flyleaf of a book she was reading: "I am now nineteen, and yet nothing of any importance has ever happened to me."

8

The heat wave was coming to an end. Far to the west the first clouds had already appeared, coming down across the shoulders of the Cuillins, then gathering slowly in a straight line across the peaks, waiting for a wind to drive them in toward the mainland. On the last evening of July, about eight o'clock, Father James took a walk up the valley to the peat loch Doonican, on the disused road which was overgrown and dusty. The high summer poppies and harebells that the sea winds shrivel grew there in thick patches and in the flat valley fields along the river. The trees were sharply separated from one another and almost flat against the sky beyond. Nothing moved in the heavy copper light; there was the kind of stillness that comes before a sudden change, as if the climate took leave of one season in a certain lull before beginning the next.

The priest felt exhausted and quite relaxed. He was so tired that his brain had lost its natural process of selection. He noticed odd pieces of rubbish in the road, once a rusty tin and later on an old shoe, as though these objects were suddenly important to him. And when a brightly colored pebble caught his eye he stopped for a moment to pick it up, thinking he had dropped something. Yet when he finally noticed Meriel Finlay, she was not more than ten feet away from him, sitting on a five-barred gate. Shock, like a shutter, closed in his brain. He stood without moving in the middle of the road and stared at her.

Meriel had watched him coming down the road. The dust flew up over his shoes, and small pebbles rattled toward the verge from under his feet. These were the only sounds in the silence of the coming storm. Sitting quietly on the gate, she had hoped he might pass her without looking up. But now the priest was staring at her as though he had walked into a trap.

"I was just sitting here," she said. "I mean—I was just going—"

Father James sighed. He was stupefied by the heat and by his own surprise. Meriel was sitting on the gate with her skirt hitched up around her thighs. From where he stood he could see all the way up her legs. The heat was now inside him, a suffocating heat that centered in his stomach and loins. He tried to disconnect himself from her, thinking of things at random, but his mind refused to focus on anything. The effort seemed too great, and he knew that sooner or later he would look at her legs again.

He cleared his throat.

"I'm sorry—I didn't hear you. Did you say you were going?"

When she answered him, he watched her mouth moving as though no sound came out of it, and yet her body seemed quite close to him. He could clearly see the freckles on her upper arms and the dust on her bare feet; and while she climbed down off the gate he shut his eyes and gave in again to the strange panic of his body, in which the blood seemed to move more swiftly and to flood into the roots of every nerve.

Meriel came up and stared at him. When he opened his eyes again she stood directly in front of him, peering anxiously into his face.

"Are you all right?" she asked. "You look very pale."

"Yes, I'm fine, thank you. It was just the heat. I'm all right now."

"You look tired. Come and sit down—there, where it's cool."

"No, I—no, thank you. I felt a little strange. Now it's gone. I must be going—it's getting dark."

Meriel was puzzled. "It won't be dark for another four hours."

"No . . . nor it will."

With an effort he walked away from her and leaned against the gate. Whether she was behind him or in front of him made no difference. He was aware of her and of nothing else. And although he gazed out across the field, a vivid and detailed picture now tormented him. He could see her naked body as clearly as though he touched it; her breasts which were round and full, the nipples pale and the veins surrounding them blue and fine beneath the skin. And her legs, of which he had just had such an excellent view, now stretched in a long slender line to the foot of his bed.

Meriel meanwhile was leaning on the gate beside him, making polite conversation in the same nervous way that a hostess would chat with an awkward guest.

". . . and when I look over there," she was saying, "toward the south, it reminds me of Edinburgh and of all the things I hate . . . imagine the typing course I'm doing, for instance—" she paused for a minute, and the priest sensed that she was looking at him. He said nothing, however, and continued to stare in a blank way at the field.

He had spent three hours driving to Lochalash hospital and three hours driving back again; he had spent two hours in the hospital wards, saying Mass behind screens, with the smell of ether in his nostrils and the sight of pain for which he could do nothing. And now, when he was vulnerable, for want of the strength to get away, he leaned on the gate beside her and listened to the sound of her voice without hearing a word she said.

If I don't leave at once, he thought, I shall be certain to touch her, first perhaps just her elbow, and then . . . and how had it happened? How had they come to be standing so close to each other? In such a place? Meriel was still talking, breaking off now and then to see if he was listening. How young she is for her age, he thought; she is still a child. And then immediately he knew that this was not the case, for this same child had the sweet, sly instincts of a grown woman. And besides this, her body gave out a direct and powerful sexuality, so that any man standing so close to her would probably feel the same physical confusion. All at once he was so exhausted that he felt a kind of anguish, an urge to clench his fists and cry out to be left alone.

Being careful not to look at her, he said at last, "You ought to go now. Your father will be wondering where you are."

She looked at him anxiously again. "You still look pale—are you sure you will be all right? I'll go now if you want me to. I only stayed—"

"No, you go—I'll be all right—it was just the heat."

But Meriel still hesitated for some reason, as though deciding whether or not to shake him by the hand, and it was the priest, at last, who turned and started to walk away from her down the road.

A little way along the dusty track he turned briefly to wave good-bye. She was perched again on the top of the gate, with her bare feet hooked under one of the bars. But the air of the coming storm seemed to thicken and grow solid around her, so that even from a short distance he could no longer see her clearly.

The priest went on with his walk, but his eyes were fixed on the road, and it was some time before he noticed that he was going in the wrong direction. Only half an hour earlier he had left the rectory in order to escape for a while from its gloomy atmosphere, and now within minutes that pretty

Georgian house which looked so inviting from the outside would enclose him again in the same stifling grip as before.

It was impossible now to turn around and go on with his walk, for Meriel Finlay was somewhere close behind him in the valley, and if he stopped for a moment he would hear her footsteps on the empty road.

The priest blamed Meriel, blamed her bitterly, for his present discontent. The more he tried to analyze the situations in which they had met, the more convinced he became that she had set out to seduce him. His first impressions of her false dreaminess and of her posing were stronger now; added to these was the strange coincidence of their meeting in the road, and even that of her confession, as parts of a single plan, perhaps begun in boredom, to infuriate and unbalance him.

During the past few weeks a subtle erosion had taken place in his state of mind; questions arose which he had never considered asking himself before, and now he longed also for the most ordinary things he had learned to do without. He started to imagine himself, for instance, sitting in the window of a coffee bar in Oxford Street, looking affectionately through the glass at those very crowds which before he had found so unremarkable. Or even of queuing for a bus and climbing up the narrow steps to the top, simply for the pleasure of lighting a cigarette. It was the mediocrity of life that he missed so unexpectedly—good food, good company— the loss of such luxuries is so tremendous that there is even a certain gaiety in giving them up. Noise, however, the useless noise of crowds and even their ugliness were things that he now needed and suddenly felt deprived of.

There was someone in whom he longed to confide. He had a cousin who was an administrator in the diocese of Salford, and whenever he wanted advice, or simply a friend to turn to, he would write to him. Now, when he thought of this, he quickened his pace in the road, and for the first time that evening, he looked up and noticed the storm that was coming in across the sound. In a little while the first rain would fall and the drought would come to an end.

When Father James went out in the evenings, Morag watched him from the rectory windows until he was out of sight. There was scarcely a time in her working day when she didn't know of his whereabouts. She had him on a string, and though it was loose-played and slack, she knew whether he went on foot or took his car, and she waited until he came back again, no matter what time of night. She watched him at ease in the rooms which did not belong to him. He slept in the dead priest's bed, and he got up in the church to give sermons on subjects which Father Macabe had never touched on.

He ill-treated her also in a number of ways. He was silent when she came into a room; he would sit with a book propped up in front of him when she served his food, and later he would leave the meal half-eaten on the plate. For each of these insults Morag had found an answer. At one time she put drops of water into the salt and shoved it onto the table in hard lumps.

"I don't know what's with it," she said. "It's nivver done that before."

The priest had merely smiled.

At another time, while she was cleaning his shoes, she put a small stone beneath the inner sole of one of them, and there was a satisfied look on her face that morning as she swept out the house and prepared his midday meal.

Although the priest scarcely seemed to notice her or to take account of her behavior, Morag had changed in subtle ways. Now she walked about the house with an unaccustomed spring in her shambling walk, and sometimes she would rest in her work and gaze at the ground in front of her with a queer, fixed smile, as though there had just then come into her head a strange and savage joke.

Sometimes when her work was finished and the priest was not at home, she would go out for a while and take a little fresh air. On such evenings when the sun still rested above the high tips of the Cuillins, and when the valley below her was drowsy and settled, Morag took from the coal shed an old deck chair which a former priest had bought in Inverness. She would drag it from the shade of the house and up the cinder path toward the churchyard. The cemetery lay under the brow of the hill, and when the late sun came down at a slant across it, the shadow of each grave was long and thin and pointed east toward the hills. It took her a certain time to get the deck chair to the foot of the cemetery, for it clattered noisily over the uneven ground and got caught among the gravestones. Down against the slope, she would lay the deck chair out, fuss a little with the angle of the seat, and settle at last to the widest view in the bay of Kintillo. On those nights when the bleating of a sheep on the far mountain slopes sounded clear and close at hand, Morag sat alert in her chair, sensitive to the slightest movement in the valley below her.

Father James that evening, was still walking slowly along the road from loch Doonican when she first noticed him. She had time without hurrying to fold the deck chair up against the wall, and when it was done she stood harmlessly by the graveyard wall, gazing at nothing with one eye, and with the other fixed on Father James.

Perhaps because her heart began to beat at a wild, irregular rate, Morag had already absorbed the shock of what she saw next before it took place.

Less than a hundred yards behind the priest, walking in her indolent way and scarcely lifting her feet off the ground, came Meriel Finlay—back down the same road that he had taken, and though she crossed the river and took a side gate into the park, Morag could see that she stopped for a minute in the road and looked up toward the rectory. And into this look she read so much guilt that Morag threw back her head and laughed aloud by the cemetery wall.

9

I'm afraid my daughters are not here," Finlay said, handing the priest a glass of sherry. "They have gone to stay with cousins in Portree."

He glanced sharply for a moment at Father James to see if he could detect a look of disappointment in his face. The priest had taken the news quite calmly, however, and even seemed relieved. He merely smiled and sipped at a little of his sherry.

"It was a terrible storm we had the other night," he said after a pause. "Several slates fell off the rectory roof."

"Terrible," Finlay agreed. He looked at his watch. "If you'll excuse me for a minute I must fetch my father from his room. And then I think we might go directly in to dinner. Since the food is cold," he added.

The priest drained his glass in a hurry and shuddered slightly, for this particular brand of sherry left a sweet and cloying taste in his mouth. The claret they drank with the meal, however, was excellent.

"Chateau Batailley '52," Sir John said loudly, turning the bottle toward him and reading out the label. "It should have been decanted.

"I remember," the old man went on, "the last time we had a bottle of this. It was in April when Magnus Laver came to dinner."

Charles Finlay put down his soup spoon in the plate. He

waited for this piece of foolishness to sink into the sudden silence.

"Doctor Laver," he said finally, "has not dined here for at least eight years."

"Well, I still remember it all the same," the old man repeated stubbornly, "and this is exactly what we drank. We had some pheasant and several bottles of the Batailley."

"I'm sorry to contradict you, Father, but I think you've confused that evening with another. This wine would have been too young to drink at the time Laver was here. He has not been inside the house for the past eight years, and on that occasion he was so drunk that he fell against the Sheraton desk in the drawing room and damaged it so badly we were unable to get it mended."

The old man was no longer listening. A bead of barley from the soup they were eating had lodged between two of his false teeth. With great patience he sucked and ferreted at this piece of barley until he had anchored it with his tongue and swallowed it.

The priest helped his host to clear away the soup plates, and presently they sat down again to some cold ham with Cumberland sauce, mashed potatoes, and Brussels sprouts. Father James was finding the evening motionless and flat, like something he was going through in his memory afterward. When he had first heard that Finlay's daughters were away, he had felt nothing but a great sense of relief. And then almost immediately in the wake of this he felt cheated. In the same way that a well-trained athlete would look forward to his next meeting with an opponent by whom he had been badly beaten, so the priest had prepared himself in advance for an evening with Meriel Finlay. He had been quite certain, moreover, of the way she would look, in the same black dress she had worn before, and by the same turns chattering and oddly silent, while he himself remained aloof and vague. With an effort he pulled himself together and was just about to speak when Charles Finlay leaned toward him and asked him if he had met the doctor yet.

"So far I haven't," he answered. "I should like to get to know him, though. The people in the village talk so much about him, don't they?"

Charles Finlay cut up the meat in his plate before replying. He speared each square rapidly with his fork and added the same amount of potato and Brussels sprouts. Finally he doused the whole forkful in Cumberland sauce before putting it into his mouth.

"I think I should warn you about the doctor," he said, and stopped.

He was going to say, "The doctor is a drunkard—it will do your reputation no good to be seen with him."

Then it occurred to him that some slight scandal involving Doctor Laver and the new young priest might be among the first small steps toward the priest's departure. Almost stealthily an idea had already formed at the back of his mind to be rid of him. Finlay wasn't used to dealing squarely with ideas of this sort; he was more inclined to chip away at them gingerly, so as not to disturb his central self-esteem.

During the meal he fiddled with the knives and forks beside his plate, as though the conversation were so boring that he could scarcely control his hands. In reality, he was quite unconscious of them. He was staring, without seeming to do so, at the priest. The first evening he had met Father James (only a month ago, but hate made him more familiar), he had looked carefully into the priest's face for some sign of warmth, but Father James had avoided this look as if it were disagreeable to him, and had averted his eyes. Charles Finlay took this as a total rejection, yet another instance of his own isolation, and during the dinner that followed (every detail of which, again by reason of his loathing, he still remembered), he had searched for and despised all the tricks of the young priest's charm. He himself was incapable of saying things he did not mean, or of laughing at jokes he did not find funny. Charm was a luxury he had been born without: it was as much of a mystery to him as any other talent he did not possess.

It's just as well my daughters are away, he thought. It's exactly this kind of empty charm that young girls find attractive.

While he stared at Father James's profile in the candle-light, a sudden idea struck him which was so obscene it made him feel giddy. For a moment he saw distinctly in front of him the spectacle of Father James making love to his daughter Anne, and the naked flesh of their buttocks and legs shone in the same candlelight he was now gazing dimly toward. Such a rage overwhelmed him that it was almost voluptuous. He closed his eyes and withdrew his hands from the table, clenching them in his lap.

At the other end of the table Sir John slept soundly. Saliva had formed a bubble in his open mouth, and this bubble went in and out with his breathing.

From time to time Charles Finlay looked at him and frowned slightly, but the meal continued and the conversation went on in the same sporadic way as before. The boredom of the whole evening now weighed on the priest to such an extent that he too was becoming drowsy, and when he fixed his eye on one of the Georgian candlesticks in front of him its silver stem began to twist about and swell oddly in the light. He had just stifled another urge to yawn when Charles Finlay rose at last to his feet.

"I'm afraid I have to take my father to bed now," he said. "When we are dining alone he is usually taken to his room a little earlier."

Father James also rose from the table, a trifle too eagerly.

"Perhaps I should go, then," he offered. "You've been very kind to ask me. It was an excellent dinner."

He looked briefly at the wine, for there was a good half bottle which remained unfinished on the table. He smiled at his host, however, and stretched out his hand to say good-bye.

Finlay shook hands with him quickly and without looking directly into his face. And a few moments later as he was showing Father James to the door, he directed such a look of loathing at his back that he wondered the young priest did not stumble under the weight of it. But Father James noticed nothing and went on down the steps into the drive. When he turned a second later to say good-bye, the great front door was already closing behind him.

I0

he priest said Mass a little earlier on Saturdays. He went down to the mail boat at nine in the morning to pick up his letters, the provisions for the church, and any parcels (sometimes books, sometimes food) sent by his family and friends. He met Magnus Laver by the boat while he was waiting for the mailbags to come out of the hold. The boat was a morning's attraction, a magnet which drew most of the villagers out of their cottages toward the pier, whether they had anything to come off it or not. There was a noise of chains and a strong smell of fish. The sea gulls flew in and out of the rigging of the boat, screaming and lunging at the decks.

Doctor Laver leaned forward and shouted something in the priest's ear. When Father James turned around he was shocked for a minute to see that the old man had no teeth.

"Will you have a drink with me, Father, in the post office?" Magnus shouted. "That is, if you don't object."

"Not at all," the priest shouted back. "I'm cold—it will do me good."

At that moment he glanced toward the boat. Meriel Finlay was getting off it, helped down the gangplank by a sailor. She wore a white Arran sweater and a scarf around her auburn hair. She looked once toward the priest and turned away. Father James felt that he stood alone, with his black cassock flapping in the wind, as conspicuous as a beacon on the top of a hill, and that every face in the parish was turned to stare in the silence not at Meriel but at him. This feeling lasted only a moment, but when he turned to follow Magnus into the post office he was cold, and his eyes smarted suddenly from the wind and from the grit on the pier.

Inside the post office, too many people were crammed into the small space, and the noise was even louder, magnified by the low ceilings and the crowded walls.

Jeanie took the two men through the flap of the counter into her little sitting room. "Pay no attention to what you hear about Doctor Laver," she said softly to the priest. "He's a good man like yourself, Father."

Magnus took a bottle and two glasses from a cupboard on the wall. "Now, you have great honesty, Jeanie." He held the bottle up to the light. "Not a single drop has been touched," he said, grinning at her.

Jeanie blushed. "I'll away and leave you in peace, then, Doctor," she said.

When she shut the door, the din from the post office receded. The glass kitchen door was also shut, but the bulk of Mrs. Mackay passed occasionally across it, reminding the priest of a great whale he had once seen circling in a tank at the London Zoo.

"Sit down, Father, sit down." Magnus pulled out two chairs and sat down to pour out the drinks. "This is not the Ritz, but it will have to do. Sometimes," he said, "when I am drunk enough, I look up from the deal table where I'm sitting and I see those potted palms and ferns against the glass, as stiff as old ladies in mourning. What a place," he sighed, still referring to the Ritz; "a tomb for kings." He wore a collarless shirt with a stud in the top of it, over which the stubble and loose flesh of his chin dropped in folds.

"Health to your parish," he said, raising his glass.

"Thank you," the priest said, smiling. "I'll drink to your health, too, and a long life."

"I don't want a long life. To tell you the truth, it's gone on too long already."

"So little to live for, have you?"

"So little—but we aren't here to discuss my troubles. This is a celebration, you see—two great minds in a little place. Mind you, I'm certain to start complaining sometime soon. The pleasure of the lonely is to store up their grievances against the day when they find a really good listener. Now you look like a really good listener."

Father James started to laugh. The unaccustomed drink had released his tension. Magnus was like a child.

"I am a good listener," he said. "Otherwise I shouldn't have become a priest."

"Now"—Magnus suddenly leaned forward, so that his nose was almost pressed against the priest's face—"I am going to ask you an impudent question that I'm certain no one in this village has had the nerve to ask you. Why should a beautiful young fellow like yourself become a priest?"

Father James flushed and folded his hands tightly in his lap.

"But the two things are not connected," he said quickly. "They have nothing to do with each other. You might just as well ask an ugly man why he is married."

"I see." Magnus was silent for a minute. He turned his glass cautiously around by the stem, between his forefinger and thumb. He looked so much like a ragged bird, perched warily on a fence, which has stolen a crumb and is waiting to see what will happen to it, that the priest began to laugh again. Magnus seemed relieved. "I'm sorry," he said. "I've grown so used to living alone, or at any rate among people who tolerate me, that sometimes I say things I've no business to."

"I don't mind. The priesthood has an odd effect on people, even the mildest people. I find that they try to shock me: if I'm asked to a dinner party, quite often there will be one or two women there wearing low-cut dresses or very short skirts. And then among the men, there will be some who swear a bit more than usual or who suddenly attack me on a moral issue they haven't cared about for years. It seems we make people feel guilty," he said with a sudden, beautiful smile, "even for no reason."

Magnus pursed his lips. "That's very true," he said gloomily, "very true. I've often noticed it."

Suddenly his face brightened. "But I will tell you a story now," he said to the priest, "in which the opposite occurs. Sometimes you will find a clergyman who takes a real delight in shocking the layman. I used to be a Catholic myself at one time and I had an uncle who was a priest."

Father James had now drunk over half a glass of neat whisky; he had a light head and was feeling a little dizzy. The doctor's features were no longer distinct. It seemed as if he were looking at him from the corner of one eye.

"This great-uncle," Magnus was saying, "was a Benedictine monk in Dublin; over ninety he was then, and with every tooth in his head. Now he was guaranteed, while sitting drinking tea in the monastery parlor with old spinsters, to start telling them of his craving for drink. It was true, this craving, and he wouldn't sit down for any length of time without returning to the topic. He would say, 'Tea is grand, Miss Flaherty—have another ginger biscuit; but usually about this time of day I am opening my second bottle of claret.' It's a fact, too, that he had at least two crates of good claret under the bed in his cell. Because of his great age, he was allowed as much wine as his relations would send him.

"Anyway, the duller"—Magnus slipped some more whisky into his empty glass—"the duller the company happened to be, the more terrible his urge to irritate them. When I was a boy of about sixteen I went to visit him once in the monastery, about the usual time for tea. There were three old maiden sisters who subscribed to the church funds there too, and, for some reason I now forget, a Protestant pastor, all at the same function. Anyhow, my uncle behaved all right for some time, eating up the sandwiches like a lamb and scarcely opening his mouth. He looked old and dim. The three spinsters were delighted, for generally he made them nervous, and they were out that day to impress the pastor with this venerable member of the Catholic Church. I was sitting there, meek and bored; my hair was slicked down with brilliantine, and I had on my best wool suit. 'It's time I was going,' said the great-uncle in the middle of a cucumber sandwich."

Father James had already started to laugh.

"No—wait," Magnus said, suppressing a hiccup. "He stood up, dusting his habit, and turned to the pastor with the nicest smile. 'Did you hear this one, Reverend,' he said, 'about the Bar Mitzvah? There was a vicar, a rabbi, and a Catholic priest—' Now, wait," Magnus said, scratching his head. "The thing is, I've forgotten the exact story now. But at any rate, no one could stop him, and he went right on until he had finished the story, and by the door he thought of another one and told them that too—all in a dead-flat voice—and the Protestant pastor spilled some hot tea in his lap, and the spinsters began to rattle and sway like trees in a gale."

Magnus became more and more Irish as the story went on, and the priest laughed so hard that he banged his elbows on the table in front of him and spilled some of his drink.

At half past twelve Jeanie knocked on the door and came in.

"Excuse me, Doctor, will you be wanting your dinner here?"

"Dinner?" said Magnus. "Ah." He squinted sideways at the whisky bottle, which was now empty. He was able still to calculate that he had drunk three-quarters of it himself.

Jeanie smiled at the priest. "Miss Morag will be waiting on you, Father, at the rectory."

"Jeanie," Magnus said, "I shall have whatever your mother is cooking there for your lunch, if you'll be so kind. It will take me just two minutes to drive Father James up the road to the rectory. We don't want to annoy Morag, do we?"

For some reason he put in his teeth to drive. It took him some time to turn the car in the village street, and then he drove at great speed up the road to the rectory, grazing the back bumper against the bridge on his way. Father James held the back door shut with a string over his shoulder.

"This car is ten years old," Magnus said. "I can't afford a new one. In general I tie that string to the knob of the windshield wiper when there is no one in the front seat beside me." He changed into low gear on the slope of the hill, and the car rocked on its axles. "You must come and see me whenever you like. Don't bother to ring. After ten o'clock at night I'm usually there."

"I should love to," said the priest. He realized that he was slightly drunk. A single terrible thought had struck him which brought him close to tears. It was literally months since he had laughed so much.

"I should love to," he said again. "I get very lonely here."

"So you must," Magnus agreed. They had arrived at the rectory by then, but neither of them made a move to get out of the car. "So you must. I get lonely too, but then, even loneliness wears a bit softer—it doesn't nag anymore—you know what I mean."

The priest nodded.

"And isn't that the terrible Morag peering at us through the window? My God, she looks as though she hadn't seen the daylight for twenty years."

Father James began to giggle. He let go the string of the back car door and struggled to get out.

"If I were you," said Magnus, leaning toward him over the seat, "I should make out I was as drunk as a barn door. Lurch in there and give her a good fright, why don't you?"

The priest laughed until he had hiccups and could scarcely catch his breath, while Magnus reversed into the garden wall and drove off down the hill in the wrong gear.

Morag turned away from the dining room window where she had been standing for the last half hour. She crossed herself. When she thought of the Devil she thought of Magnus Laver.

For several days Father James avoided the doctor. Magnus had the same effect on him as alcohol: there was a sweet warmth about him, and a peculiar sense of danger. In exactly the same way as strong drink alters the outward eye, confusing and even doubling its vision, so Magnus worked on the inner, setting up a false set of standards and half-truths. Yet the priest in his loneliness felt a longing for the doctor's company, and after a while he gave in to it. He set off up the road one night about ten o'clock. It was five miles from Kintillo to Toscaig, and the priest drove slowly and almost reluctantly. The sky was clear after a day of rain. The full moon shone at a slant on the puddles in the road, which looked as white and dense as solid ice.

The doctor's cottage looked deserted—no light showed through the windows, and the glass shone blind in the moonlight. Father James climbed the steep hill. He decided to look through a window before knocking on the door, hoping to see a sign that Magnus was still about.

There, less than three feet from his own face through the glass, sat Magnus Laver, staring out at him without a flicker of recognition. Nothing in his face moved; his skin was dead white in the light of the moon. Starting backward, Father James stumbled against a bucket by the doorway. Angrily he straightened the bucket, rubbing his shin where he had grazed it on the rim. As he opened the door Magnus started to laugh.

"Did you think I was mummified with drink, Father?"

"You startled me," the priest said sharply. "What on earth are you doing sitting here in the dark?"

Magnus rubbed his hands across his eyes and yawned. "No, the truth of the matter is I nearly got it."

"Got what?"

In the mess that littered the tables and chairs, the priest was feeling about for some kind of light, a lamp or even a candle. He was sorry by now that he had come.

Magnus was still staring out of the window and seemed only half removed from his trance. "Isn't it always the same?" he said peacefully. "Just as you are reaching out and the thing is coming at you full face and clear—in this godforsaken place, where a mouse moving is a big event, someone always has to walk in on you."

Father James had found a candle and some matches. He lit the candle and set it down in a saucer and then looked at Magnus.

"And I bet you haven't eaten anything all day," he said. "Are you trying to starve yourself to death?" Magnus annoyed him so much at that moment that he searched around for something more insulting to say. "Look at all those bottles"—he made a sweep with his arm and knocked it against the sharp corner of the paraffin stove. "At least, if I were you—"

Magnus interrupted him. "How rude of me, Father," he said. "I haven't offered you a drink."

Father James had already made a resolution not to touch any alcohol that night with Magnus. He had intended to sit there for an hour or so, talking, and then drive home; but he was so irritated by then, and the cold was so intense, that he took the drink Magnus held out to him and swallowed three mouthfuls neat.

After he had tipped a whole glass of whisky down his own

throat and lit up a cheap cigar, Magnus pulled himself slowly from his chair, and between them they lit the fire, which threw up a choking cloud of smoke, and drew the curtains shut. By the soft light of three candles and by the deeper light of the fire the sharp angles and the squalor of the room dissolved, and the setting seemed right, as nowhere else, for the doctor's strange and lengthy monologues.

"Ah, that's good," he said, settling back in his chair. "My God, I don't miss electric light, and if it weren't for the drafts in this place, I should call it perfect."

The priest agreed. He was already ashamed of his previous bad temper, and at the same time he was reluctant to destroy the sudden atmosphere of intimacy by apologizing for it. "When I came in," he said, "you were saying something— I've forgotten exactly what it was—you said something about finding it—finding what?"

"Ah," said Magnus. He shifted slightly in his chair. For an instant he looked coy, and this expression on his dissipated face startled the priest.

"Well, I'll try to explain it to you," he said. "People ask me periodically why I drink so much. I give each of them a different answer—to keep warm, to keep alive, to die quicker, what have you. The same people who ask this kind of personal question seem satisfied with the same banal answers, you see—"

Father James nodded and sipped a little more of his drink. The doctor's voice, the gradual warmth of the peat fire, and the pale, waxy light of the candles all had the same soothing quality.

"Well, now—there are better reasons than that for drinking. I might have used drugs instead, if I could have afforded them." Magnus leaned forward in his chair. "But it comes to the same. I need a stimulant these days to get at what I'm after, and of course it takes more all the time. I'll try to explain it to you. Do you ever have the peculiar sensation, Father, that you have hold of something—not an idea, but a very perfect dream, a kind of visible ecstasy—and that you just have hold of it by the corner; and say you try to examine it or to keep it there even for a few minutes, but you can't, because it won't take the strain—it fades completely, and there is nothing left of it but a sense of terrible loss—"

Again the priest nodded. He was thinking, This is all nonsense, of course, but at the same time he was mesmerized by the doctor's eyes and voice.

"Well," Magnus went on, "if I could only produce this strange kind of rapture when I wanted it and stay with it sometimes for a while as I used to do—for instance, when I was young, still a child, when sometimes I was so unhappy and there was nothing anybody could do about it, this unhappiness was often accompanied by a certain picture in my mind, and this was so vivid that I was often able to weep for half an hour as a result of it. And yet it was a meaningless little scene, in no way connected with me, of a man in a raincoat walking away down a dark road at night, with his hands in his pockets, hunched up against the rain. This beating rain fell through the lamp-lit circles in the road, and overhead the weak light lit up the leaves of interminable plane trees. The stranger was walking away down the road so slowly that he never seemed to move. . . ."

Into this—with Magnus half whispering, half sunk already into a coma, and the priest staring at him, leaning forward in his chair—into this mist of Magnus Laver's great confusion, there came a sudden knocking on the door. The sound was so totally unexpected that the two men sat staring at each other until the knocking began again. The priest sighed and put down his empty glass. Magnus went slowly to the door and opened it.

"Oh, it's you, is it?" he said. "If it was anybody else I should have left them out in the cold—come in, then."

Even before he heard her voice the priest realized that it was Meriel Finlay.

She came quickly into the room, pulled off her headscarf and brushed her hair back from her face. She apologized to Magnus for disturbing him and at the same time she smiled at him gaily. And she was so busy with all of this that she failed to notice the priest until she had sat down.

Magnus hung up her coat on a peg by the door. He turned to offer Meriel a drink and stopped there with his mouth ha'f open. The priest and Meriel Finlay were staring at each other in such a way that he, Magnus, was now alone in the room. Two things happened at once to him. An intolerable pain attacked him somewhere in the region of his heart, forcing him to sit down quickly in a chair, and at the same moment he thought quite clearly, The two of them are lovers; they have been lovers for some considerable time. Furthermore, he could see that the whole evening was planned. Neither of them had come to see him at all.

"Of course," he said suddenly, loudly, "you know each other already."

Meriel turned in her chair. She put her hand quickly over her mouth as though she were covering a smile or even a desire to laugh. Behind her the priest stood up and walked toward the fire, spreading out his hands to the flames, although the room was now so warm that Magnus felt stifled.

"I'm hungry," Magnus complained. "I think I need something to eat—in fact I haven't eaten all day."

"I'll help you," Meriel said. "What shall I cook you?"

"Don't trouble yourself on my account. I should hope that I can open a tin without someone rushing to help me. I am definitely not so drunk, am I, that I can't open a tin by myself?"

Meriel shrugged. "How queer you are tonight," she said. "Have I done something wrong? I can't think—perhaps I shouldn't have come—I walked five miles up the road to see you. I thought you would be pleased."

Magnus ignored her. He went to a cupboard by the sink where he kept cardboard boxes full of whisky. He drew the cork out of one with a sharp twist and drank straight from the bottle.

"Christ," he said. "Now, I needed that."

But again neither Meriel nor the priest was paying attention to him. Without even looking at each other they were surrounded by a physical confusion from which he was totally excluded. He watched them for a minute with his eyes narrowed and the whisky bottle still in one slack hand, then he turned back toward the sink where he was standing, picked up a box of matches, opened it, and deliberately scattered the contents on the floor. "Now look what's happened," he said plaintively. The two of them came across the room to pick up the matches and knelt down and gathered them together in silence. Meriel was on one knee sweeping the matches into piles, and whenever she stretched forward her hair brushed against the priest's face. And when she touched Father James, he shut his eyes and turned his face slightly toward her. When he straightened up he took Meriel by the arm and helped her to her feet, and Magnus saw too that she stumbled against him, pressing the side of her breast against his hand.

When all the matches were back in their box on a table, Magnus sat down again and crossed one leg over the other.

"I am going to write this book," he said at random. "Have I told you about it, Father?" The priest was staring at the contents of his glass, swilling it around in one hand, and when he looked up it was neither directly at the doctor's face nor at Meriel Finlay but somewhere among the shadows between the two of them. Magnus wondered how long it would be his pleasure to bore his two guests. He watched them shrewdly in the same way that a teacher might watch his class toward the end of the lesson, noting whose eyes had strayed toward the classroom clock and who was paying attention.

"I've decided to call this book *The Mindwatcher*," he went on. "It will be the study of an alcoholic examining his own brain, you see, watching its gradual dissolution. Step by step now, from the time that the disease first takes hold of him—beginning with those great bursts of sunlight that are so beguiling at first, and those dreams which are so rich and bright that you can practically reach out and touch them. And then describing after a time the slow festering of these same dreams, the slow dissolving into nightmares. . . ."

The worst of this monologue, the doctor now realized, was that it produced no effect on his listeners at all, not even the desire to yawn.

"Such nightmares," he went on, raising his voice, "that presently descend from the head, you see, into the pit of the stomach, and here they crawl about like worms. Sometimes I have woken up, clutching my stomach, certain that there was a hole there from which these worms were oozing and wriggling out. Doesn't this revolt you?" he said, suddenly leaning toward Meriel.

"Who, me?" she said, looking up. She had been picking at the loose varnish on the wooden arm of her chair. With an effort she roused herself and smiled at him. "I forgot," she said. "You haven't eaten yet. Shall I cook you something?"

She is radiant, he thought. I have never seen her look so beautiful.

"Shall I make you an omelette? It won't take me a minute."

Magnus took some more whisky, and while he was doing this he stared sideways at her over the upraised bottle.

"Or a bacon sandwich—something you really like?"

"No," he said abruptly. "No, thank you—I'm not hungry anymore. I think I'll go to bed now, if you don't object."

No one made a move to stop him. The other two people in the room were in that strange stage which prevented them from understanding anything the doctor said unless he spoke loudly or repeated himself.

"I think I'll go to bed," he said again.

Father James stirred in his chair. "Yes," he said, "why don't you? I was going to take Meriel home anyway—it's getting late."

He leaned forward to blow out a candle that was guttering in its saucer. It was only the second time he had spoken since Meriel had walked through the door.

Magnus had no intention of going to bed. As far as he was concerned, most of the night was still ahead of him—it was certain now to be a long dull night, and lonely too, intolerably lonely. He felt the same pain as before. It was settling now in the pit of his stomach, merely waiting until the door shut, and in the silence it would stir up a storm inside him.

"Must you go?" he said suddenly.

His voice was so feeble that Meriel looked at him anxiously.

"Don't you want us to?"

In spite of the way she spoke, Magnus realized that there was no way to delay her; she had made up her mind to leave with the priest. He shrugged.

"Well, if you're going to leave," he said, "why don't you leave? The fire is going out. The room's getting cold. I shall have to warm it up again when you've gone."

The priest had already put on his coat and was helping

Meriel into hers. In a sense they had already left. He closed his eyes for a second, refusing to think what they might do together once they had shut his door.

"Good night, Magnus." Meriel crossed the room and kissed him lightly on the cheek. "I'll come again soon. Look after yourself."

Magnus said nothing. He was watching the priest by the doorway. Even in the warm light Father James looked pale and half asleep.

When they had gone, Magnus stayed where he was for a while, leaning against the stove. Suddenly, as though they mattered now, he remembered two things: in one hand, already stiff, he was still holding the whisky bottle. The second was more disgraceful: in the ten years that he had known Meriel Finlay she had never seen him, until that night, without his teeth.

Father James drove for a mile or so in silence. It was starting to rain again—thick clouds flew across the moon, pushed by a violent wind which shook the car and scattered the rain against the windows. Meriel sat beside the priest, watching the trees and solitary houses slip past along the road. Each of those that stood out against the night was a landmark she knew well, and by each she worked out how little time she had left. There was so great a step between her desire and its fulfillment that Meriel sat dumbly in her seat and wondered how it could ever be accomplished. By a flat stretch of empty land between Toscaig and Kintillo, where the steep flank of the hills fell away on one side into a landlocked pool and where the beach came up on the other side to a smooth green ridge of grass, Meriel said suddenly:

"Won't you stop the car for a minute before I have to go home?"

The priest cleared his throat. "Now listen to me, Meriel."

"I'm listening—"

He sighed. He stopped the car by the side of the road, and when he turned toward her, Meriel was looking at him, sitting quite still with her hands in her lap.

Her scarf was tied too tightly around her head, and the priest leaned forward to loosen it. He ran one hand lightly through her hair and around the nape of her neck beneath it. She leaned against him so that he might kiss her, but the priest brushed her skin with his lips, her eyelids, the hollows of her temples and neck, the small round flesh of one earlobe, and this so lightly that Meriel put her arms around his neck and kissed him on the mouth. In that darkness where the blood is pumped faster out of the heart, among the veins which open wider to flood it through every nerve, beneath the skin which inch by inch wakes up, the body burns for use and the brain alone seems to sleep. Meriel heard one meaningless sound in that darkness, the clicking of the windshield wipers which the priest had forgotten to switch off.

She unbuttoned her coat so that he might touch her breasts. And she tormented him by leaning her head far back against the seat so that he had another six inches of her flesh to kiss, down into the collar of her dress. While he was kissing her, she took his head in her hands and ran her fingers through his hair. And later she allowed him to undo her dress, which was fastened down the front by an ornamental zipper. But the zipper caught before it was halfway down, and here unaccountably Father James turned away from her. He straightened up in the seat, and presently he leaned forward and rested his head against the steering wheel. In the dim white reflection of the headlights on the road Meriel watched him. She looked at his ruffled hair and listened to the sound of his rapid breathing because these were the extensions of her own desire.

After a few minutes he said, "Please do up your dress again. I can't look at you."

For the first time Meriel noticed the cold. The neck of her dress was wide open and the cleft between her breasts was visible above the broken zipper. She buttoned up her coat and sighed.

"I wish—" she began.

Father James refused to look at her, even with her coat buttoned up to the chin. He gazed at the road ahead as though the answer to something lay there beyond the beam of the headlights in the darkness.

"I wish it too," he said. "I wish we had never met." They were speaking, however, of different things. "I'll take you home now . . . and afterward you must try not to think of me nor to see me again before you go home. You must forget about me altogether—you must do this for yourself and also for me."

12

Meriel spent most of her time alone, sometimes walking in the bare hills around the Kintillo valley, taking the long straight paths through the forestry plantations where the larch needles fell in a steady rain about her feet. Throughout these long walks, she noticed nothing around her. She was totally absorbed by herself and by the priest. She reminded herself continually that from one year's end to the next she would not see him, but her misery at these times would bewilder her, because, in spite of everything, it reminded her of an overwhelming happiness.

At least once a day she went down to the post office, and she would settle herself on a corner of the counter between the sweets display and the till. From this position she could see the priest either coming down the rectory hill or walking in the village street. It was remarkable, however, that considering the time she spent there, he did not once appear.

Occasionally she would fix the postmistress with a careful look and begin to talk in such a way as to draw the conversation gradually toward Father James.

"I wonder," she would say, "how anyone can stand to be a priest? It must be so intolerably lonely."

"I don't know altogether," Jeanie would answer. "Certain though, it must be lonely," and she would leave it at that.

On one occasion Meriel said, "And why should any man give up the chance to have a wife and children? And to lead a normal life?"

The postmistress had never considered such questions as these.

"Surely I nivver thought of it," she said in a puzzled voice. "Maybe there are those who don't need such things, though, for we're none of us made the same." And presently she went on with her work.

One morning while Meriel was there, certain to miss Father James again because his car was no longer by the rectory door or parked in the village street, Magnus Laver came into the shop. He managed to ignore Meriel, although he walked within inches of her to get to the middle of the counter.

"Jeanie," he said, leaning forward with the two rows of his teeth put in for the occasion, "good morning."

"Good morning, Doctor," said Jeanie, smiling. She was cleaning the counter with a damp cloth. "What can I do for you?"

"Since the pub is not yet open, may I trouble you for a quart bottle of pale ale?"

"You'll be wanting to sit next door, then—I'll away in there and see if the stove is lit."

"Don't trouble yourself," Magnus said gently. "I'm quite warm enough, thank you. Meriel," he said, turning so sharply that his elbow caught her on the arm, "will you do me the honor of sitting for a while next door with me? It's a lonely thing for a man to be drinking entirely by himself."

Meriel nodded without a word and slid down off the countertop.

"Good, then," the doctor said, rubbing his hands. "Good, good."

Without seeming to do so, he was watching the ale froth up toward the rim of the mug and feeling in his hip pocket for the flask containing the whisky which he would later add to spice it up a little.

He held the door open for Meriel behind the counter and followed her into the room, taking care to keep the brimming mug steady in his one free hand. Meriel sat down on the window seat with her back to the light, and Magnus sat down a little way to the side of her where he could look into her face. He set the bottle and the mug of ale gently on the table and sighed. That morning Meriel sensed a meanness in him. He had changed in the summer since she had come home; there was sharpness, a certain malice in the doctor now which had never been there before. She sat silent, her hands in her lap.

"Well," Magnus said, after he had taken a good quarter of a pint, "how long is it now until you leave? A week? Ten days?"

Meriel cleared her throat. "No," she said. "Tomorrow."

Magnus clicked his teeth together and sighed again.

"Ah," he said. "Tomorrow."

When she heard these words from someone else, though she had been saying the same thing to herself since the early morning, a blind rush of tears filled her eyes, and she stared at the floor while these tears brimmed over and hung from her lower lashes.

"Don't cry," Magnus said briskly. "What you need, Meriel, is a course of vitamin B_{12} injections—for the nerves, you see. Now, the food you eat in this place is insipid stuff, overcooked and without an ounce of real content in it. Not that I eat much myself, but then you don't have the benefit of alcohol, do you? Which reminds me—" He removed the flask of whisky from his pocket and slipped a little into his ale. "Here, have some of this," he said, holding out the flask. "It will cheer you up."

Meriel shook her head.

They sat for a while without talking. When she could bear this silence no longer, since it was full of implications, and since Magnus seemed happy to sit there and enjoy her discomfort, Meriel began to talk at random.

"Anyway," she said, "Anne will be glad to leave. She has this boyfriend, a student doctor, back in Edinburgh, who's always writing to her. I shouldn't be surprised if he's the kind of man she marries—I mean, eventually."

"Mmmmm," Magnus said loudly. He pinched an earlobe between his finger and thumb, pulling the flesh downward until it was stretched grotesquely out of shape.

"She wants," Meriel went on, turning slightly away from him, "a neat terraced house in Edinburgh, with a patio at the back, two children, and a three-week holiday abroad every summer."

"Not, I gather, your Shangri-la," Magnus said, again loudly, as if he were deaf and could no longer hear the sound of his own voice.

"No—no, it's not. The trouble is, I don't know what I want—but it's not that, at least. That would be like building your own prison, wouldn't it? Did you ever think, Magnus, how many times in one year you could be locking yourself in and out of the same little house—say four times a day, three hundred and sixty-five days a year—and even away from it you would still be taking practically the same tracks every time. You would wear out hundreds of pairs of shoes on the same pavements, year after year."

"Some people must earn their living; they have no choice," Magnus said heavily. He was staring at the fireplace, above which hung a little wooden plaque that Meriel had never noticed before. Into the wood of this plaque had been burned the words *Home, Sweet Home* in slanting print, and the motto was surrounded by painted roses and stray leaves. There was a sickly smell of paraffin in the room from the unlit stove.

"It's the way you were brought up, Meriel," Magnus said

after a pause, "by the puritan aunt and uncle. The straight and narrow was never any good for those with hot blood in their veins. In the end, that kind of life is only something to kick against, a barrier between yourself and reality. They never teach you, for instance, that there's such a word as money, stuff to fling around when you get the chance and enjoy a bit. It's a life of toil behind the net curtains, and the money is saved against the day of wrath. It's a sin to spend it and a misdemeanor to smile on Sunday and the Good Book is entirely without humor, isn't it? There's no such word in this vocabulary as joy, or hilarity, or even nonsense. My God," he said, "when you have no sense of humor, what a steep hill this life must be, don't you think?"

Meriel smiled. "They're not really as bad as that," she said timidly.

"Ah, but what fine, upright, dutiful people. I remember them coming here once to the village store—the only time, to my knowledge, they've been to Kintillo since your mother died—"

"They brought us back from school one summer on their way to Inverness."

"Yes—well, your aunt marched into the post office before she would put a foot through the lodge gates. 'Is my brother-in-law at home, Mistress Mackenzie?' she said to Jeanie." Magnus pronounced the word "Mistress" with a sharp hissing sound that shifted his false teeth. "Now, Jeanie had just the time to nod when your aunt, with a swish of her foxtail attachments, was out of the door again and ordering the trunks put down in the village street.

" 'Would you like a cup of tea, Mrs. Graham?' Jeanie said from the doorway.

" 'No, thank you,' said the aunt, halfway back to the car again. 'We haven't the time to wait, have we, Thomas?' Through all this your uncle had never so much as opened his mouth until he said good-bye to you, and they were gone before I had time to get the whisky glass back to my mouth from the counter."

Meriel looked at him gravely. She was scarcely listening to him, having been there herself at the time, and having heard the story before both when Magnus was drunk and when he was sober. It seemed as if a sudden block of ice had settled around her heart, and now when she spoke she was afraid that her words might sound heavy with self-pity.

"You know, in the whole of my life—" she began in a trembling voice. Magnus said nothing, but he focused on her with an odd air of delicacy.

"In the whole of my life," she repeated, "I've never seen a photograph of my mother. I can't imagine her. When I think—when I try to see her in my mind, there is just this blank where her face should be, and then, though her hair is short, her body is thin and bony like mine. I've no idea what she was really like."

"Well," Magnus said, sighing, "I'm afraid I don't know either. She died before I came here—a good few years before, but I think she did look like you—smaller perhaps, more languorous and plump." He spread out his hands on the table with the palms downward and gazed at them intently, lifting each finger separately an inch or so from the surface. He was passing the time until he could change the subject. "What I never understood about your family," he said finally, "is the rift between them after your mother's death. It's quite beyond me how people can be so foolish. I've never understood whether it was caused by your father, or whether it was the aunt." Magnus spoke of this aunt with bitterness, as though she had done him a personal wrong. "She who refused to speak to your father—on account of what," he added briskly, "I neither know nor care."

"Well," said Meriel. She was moving an ashtray around

with the tip of her finger, there being nothing else on the table to fiddle with. "I think she always held it against him—the way that my mother died."

"What!" Magnus shouted. He slammed his hand down so hard on the table that the ale bottle jumped and Meriel put out a hand to save it.

"I've never heard so much rubbish in my life—would you credit it? Your poor mother died of a hemorrhage after childbirth. Do you mean to tell me that the aunt has arranged the thing in her head in such a way that your father is to blame for it? My God—what a wicked, senseless woman."

"It wasn't quite that," Meriel said, even more timidly. "I think she blamed my father for not getting hold of the doctor sooner—"

"So what is she?" cried Magnus, getting more and more incensed. "A self-elected gynecologist? What did she know about childbirth, being as I remember totally infertile herself? Huh!"

With impatience, he shook the remaining few drops from the quart bottle into his mug. Meriel regretted having spoken at all. It was typical of the doctor that no sooner had he heard something of this sort, and no sooner had he taken enough alcohol, than he became more outraged and more involved in it than the person affected, not only removing from them some of their own just grievances but even putting them into the position of defending the very thing that had made them angry.

"Now look, Magnus," Meriel said firmly, "she has never once mentioned the subject. I don't even know if—"

"My God, I should hope not!" cried Magnus, again slamming the table. "Of all the narrow-minded, misinformed, merciless bitches I have ever in my long life heard mentioned— Be so good, my child," he said suddenly, "as to fetch me another quart bottle of pale ale from next door—the Whitbreads, please. When I hear of such bigotry and meanness it has a terrible effect on my thirst—"

When Meriel came back with the bottle already opened and the froth running down over her fingers, Magnus looked up at her as though she had just come into the room for the first time. When she put the bottle down on the table, he thanked her gravely and poured and swallowed a· whole mugful without pausing for breath.

"So," he said finally, squaring his shoulders and planting his hands firmly on either side of the mug, "it's about time you acquired a taste for a bit of living—you owe it to yourself, really."

"A bit of living?" Meriel repeated. She shifted on the window seat slightly farther away from Magnus. "A bit of living? What do you mean?"

"What should I mean?" said the doctor vaguely. "Really nothing." He turned sideways to gaze out of the window, and Meriel noticed that he hadn't shaved for at least two days.

"Ah," he said, "I see your sister Anne coming up the village street. 'Sister Anne, Sister Anne,' he sang suddenly in a strange falsetto voice, "who do you see there coming down the road in the dust? . . ."

The two of them sat in silence, like conspirators savoring the last minutes of a certain freedom. Magnus began to pick his nose, furtively and at the same time stubbornly. Anne Finlay came through the sitting room door with a firm step. Her eyebrows were raised and her eyes accusing.

"Magnus," she said briskly, "I'm sorry for interrupting you. I'm to bring you home to finish packing," she said to Meriel.

A great draft of fresh air came in through the door behind her and Magnus began to grumble, pulling his coat collar up around his ears.

"The very same as her aunt," he muttered.

Anne had a hand on her hip and was looking at Meriel in such a way as to say, "Another minute in this beer-ridden atmosphere will be too much for me."

"I'm coming," Meriel said absent-mindedly. She had been struck just then by an idea so simple and at the same time so brilliant that she almost choked with laughter. She gave the doctor a radiant smile and kissed him on the cheek. "I must go," she said.

Magnus had hold of her by one arm and refused to let go.

"I was telling your sister," he said to Anne, "I was telling her to live it up a bit in the black sour streets of Edinburgh. Get dancing with the students in the bars, why don't you? My God, at your age I was maddened by sex." He hiccupped. "Excuse me—and bearing in mind the dull clothes they wore then in those days, I couldn't look at a pair of pretty ankles without the blood rushing to my head. Are you going, then?"

"Good-bye, Magnus—I'll try to come to see you before I go." Meriel was impatient to leave. She longed to be alone now and to study this new idea which had come to her with such suddenness that she felt almost giddy.

"Let's go," she said to Anne. "Come on, let's go."

Magnus looked up at her suspiciously as she left the room, but the sustained effort of staring at Meriel, with both eyes at once, distressed him. As they shut the door the doctor began to sing again in the same weary falsetto he had used a few minutes before, pulling the empty beer mug around and around by the handle.

13

Every evening Charles Finlay went to bed at ten o'clock, having first bolted the front door and checked the shutters of every ground-floor room. Since it was built in 1720 the house had never been burglarized, but he did these things out of habit. It was part of his army training that he liked every lock and bolt in working order, well oiled and sliding easily into place. It had never once occurred to him that everything he was doing he had done a hundred thousand times before, and always in the same order throughout the long monotonous years.

When the last light on the ground floor had been switched off, he went upstairs to his room. Halfway up the stairs he stopped and an expression of fear passed over his face. There was a light beneath his bedroom door, and this light shone out boldly in the semidarkness.

In all the years since his wife's death, no one other than the housemaids had crossed the threshold of his room. Throughout those years Charles Finlay had built around himself a tight and fussy routine, so that one single breach in it caused him the degree of terror a normal man would feel if the foundations of his house began to shift beneath his feet.

He walked softly up the last few steps of the stairs, one hand in his pocket. He had some wild notion of bringing out his stiletto and brandishing it in the face of the intruder. It did not occur to him that one of his daughters might be waiting in his room for him, and when he opened the door and saw Meriel sitting quietly on his bed, he stood rigidly in the doorway and could think of nothing whatsoever to say to her. Meriel also sat without speaking, staring up at him with frightened eyes.

"Papa," she began.

But the setting was strange to her. Not only the expression in her father's face, but the whole atmosphere of the room now so terrified her that the phrases she had been planning throughout the day stuck in her dry throat. Ever since the morning when she had first conceived her plan, sitting in the store with Magnus, she had put off mentioning it to her father. Each time an opportunity had arisen, she had somehow avoided it. And she had reached, by this indecision, the worst possible moment of all, so that she now sat wretchedly on the bed and stared at him as though she were dumb.

Finlay had meanwhile recovered sufficiently to come into the room and close the door behind him. He took a clean handkerchief from his trouser pocket, blew his nose loudly in it and rearranged it, without thinking, in the breast pocket of his jacket. He then made an extraordinary remark.

"I hope," he said somberly, "that you haven't been meddling with my gun."

Meriel was astonished. "Your gun?"

"You must have noticed it," he went on. "In the corner over there. It's not loaded, but I don't like it tampered with. Besides," he added, "fingerprints leave acid marks on the barrels."

"What do you need a gun for?" she said wonderingly. "I mean, in here?"

"In the summer the tomcats come down from the home farm and prowl about the park. You must have noticed them—"

"Noticed them? No, not specially."

"I find that extraordinary," Finlay said, staring at her, "considering the noise they make, night after night—and just beneath the windows, too, when one is trying to get some sleep."

The conversation now resembled a scene on a darkened stage, a scene in which the dialogue of the principal actors has flown over the heads of the audience and into some dim region of the playwright's fancy.

"I suppose I hear them," Meriel said after a pause. "I suppose sometimes I do—but do you kill them?" she asked suddenly.

"Kill them? Certainly I do. Besides the infernal noise they make, they have no business down here in the woods. They disturb the young pheasants."

"I see."

If she closed her eyes, there was a small vivid picture in her mind: she could see the thin carcass of a cat stretched out in the twilight, pale against the dark grass.

"Why did you want to see me?"

Finlay had now sat down on a straight-backed chair by the door and crossed his legs. Meriel began to fidget. She avoided looking at him.

"I don't want to go back to Edinburgh tomorrow," she said hurriedly. "I want to stay here, at home—"

For the second time that evening Finlay gazed at his daughter as though she were a stranger whose thoughts and actions were quite inexplicable to him. He took so long to reply that Meriel was afraid he had not understood her.

"If I stay here, I could look after you," she said. "You and Grandpapa."

"And do you really want to stay here alone while Anne goes back to Edinburgh?"

"I've spoken to her about it. She doesn't mind what I do. She's happy to go back; she likes her work, her friends—she has a whole life there, while I—"

"Well," Finlay said in a measured way, "within a week you will be bored."

"I won't be, I promise you. I shall find plenty to do."

Meriel blushed, for it was here that her thoughts divided into two quite separate streams. They were not definite enough to be counted as plans. On the one hand she meant to look after her father and to keep him company in ways that still remained vague to her, and on the other she wished simply to be near the priest. It was for the second of these two reasons that she now blushed deeply.

Finlay got up and began to walk about the room. Out of his pocket he drew a small knife which he drummed in a military tattoo against the palm of his hand.

"What about your typing course?"

"I've almost finished it. And then—well, I could go out tomorrow and get a job as a secretary."

"I don't think you have the natural efficiency for such a job."

There was no denying it. Meriel said nothing.

"And I suppose you have considered what your aunt will have to say?"

She shrugged. "I don't think she cares very much one way or the other."

Finley stopped fiddling with the knife and slipped it back into his pocket.

"You would be a fool to imagine it," he said crisply. "She has plans for you. I've no doubt she would like to see you, with your looks and education, married to a peer of the realm, mmm?

"Whereas," he continued, before she could speak, "here you will have nothing to do and will meet no one—"

"I won't mind."

"You won't mind?"

He seemed incredulous. He stared at her face intently, as though he had just then made out certain facts which she was trying to conceal from him. Meriel wanted terribly to cry. The whole conversation from the very beginning had set off at some crazy slant, and this slant had never been corrected again. It had been foolish of her to imagine that her father would be delighted, or even interested in her scheme. When she considered it, she had only once in the past summer seen such an expression in his face, and this was when his head keeper, Mackinnon, had trapped and killed in the mouth of the river a great bull seal that was eating the heads off his salmon.

She got up from the bed and straightened up the covers. "If you don't want me to stay, Papa, I'll go—tomorrow, with Anne."

These words, however, sounded clumsy and self-pitying, and they seemed also to bring the conversation to a sudden end, so that she was surprised when her father spoke again.

"If," he said abruptly, "you would really like to stay, I see no reason why you shouldn't. Some short interval, say six months or even a year, and then we shall see—"

The tears which Meriel had tried so hard to control now ran down her face unchecked. And Finlay, at the sight of these tears, immediately withdrew again into his normal state of cold reserve. He managed to push Meriel toward the door, holding her gingerly by one arm, but even this slight contact seemed disagreeable to him. In the open doorway, sensing that she was about to thank him, or, even worse, to lean forward to kiss him on the cheek, Finlay turned away from her hurriedly and switched on the passage light.

"You had better go now," he said quickly. "There's nothing more to be said."

As soon as he had shut the door and was alone again, he began to walk restlessly up and down the room. At first he was struck merely by the unreality of the situation. He walked up and down the same stretch of floor, bounded at one end by the bed and at the other by the window, and from time to time he looked up and stared at the familiar objects in the room around him—the finely carved handles of his chest of drawers, the frame of a picture which hung above his bed. These things now seemed filled with a fresh significance. The sudden shock had disturbed his sense of balance, sharpening certain faculties and blunting others, so that twice, out of habit, he went to the windows to draw the curtains, and each time he turned away again, forgetting at the last minute why he was there.

While he undressed, he took from his wallet the two photographs he kept of his daughters. Selecting the one of Meriel, he stared at it greedily, as though he were hoping to find sudden traces of affection in the stilted face which gazed back at him.

And later when he had turned out the light, he lay for some time without closing his eyes. Something strange and almost luxurious disturbed him—a happiness so intense that he treated it warily. This feeling was quite foreign to him. When he thought of it, there had been only one occasion in the past few years when he could remember anything like it. And this had been on a morning in late October when there was a heavy frost on the ground. The sun had drawn out the colors of the autumn woods so that every tree and bush seemed to blaze with a cold and brilliant fire. Finlay had taken his gun with him and a new young Labrador, Victory. In the hard-frozen stubble of the open fields, the untrained gun dog had put up a great cock pheasant. Finlay, at a distance of one hundred fifty yards, had raised his gun and shot this splendid bird straight through the chest. And as he watched his prey fall from the sky in a straight line to the ground, a feeling of pleasure and intense surprise had overcome him. He smiled to himself in the darkness. This was what he now felt: complete surprise, the sense that one has been given a totally unexpected gift. He yawned loudly, turned over in the bed, and settled himself to sleep.

I4

When Anne had gone, the house settled again into an almost total silence. Outside in the park could be heard the grating cry of the rooks and the changing sound of the sea and the wind, but the inside of the house seemed empty and almost lifeless. In a number of small ways Meriel missed her sister, and although these ways were negative (for they seldom spoke to each other or did anything together), the loss was unexpected and troublesome.

At first she had waited for a sense of change to take place in her, for the threads of her three lives—the school, the city, and her father's house—were drawn together in a single place and now ran together. But this one life was at times as tedious and undirected as the other three.

After a week of rain, the weather had settled again. The air was unusually sweet and warm, and one morning when Meriel went out, there was a treacherous smell of fresh-trodden grass and earth that reminded her of spring. She began to walk, for no reason, toward the home farm. She had noticed that the priest's car was no longer outside the rectory door, and thus the morning, from being lightened by many possibilities, took on a single heavy density so that she was bored already and dispirited.

Some way ahead of her she now noticed a sick sheep lying in the middle of the road. It had been lying there for some time, unable to move, and at Meriel's approach the animal gazed up at her with an expression of suffering that was oddly human. As she stepped around it, she shuddered. It occurred to her that it was about to die and that its great head might suddenly loll forward and brush the side of her legs.

She was twenty yards from the entrance to the home farm, and Mrs. Mackinnon, the housekeeper, was now coming toward her with a basket on one arm.

"Look at that poor sheep." Meriel said to her as she approached. "Someone should put it out of its misery."

Mrs. Mackinnon shook her head.

"It's that softie Morrison," she said, referring to the head shepherd. "He cannot bear to put a bullet into anything. I have here," she continued tranquilly, "a nice cake for your father's tea. It was freshly baked this morning."

She lifted the lid of a round tin inside her basket and surveyed the brown crust of the cake.

"I always think a fresh cake looks nice. I don't like the cellophane they put on things these days. It gives them the queer unnatural look of the factory."

Meriel agreed. She too looked at the cake, which gave off a sharp, delicate smell of raisins and warm baking. A question had just then formed in her mind, however, and at once became so urgent that it was out of her mouth before she could stop it.

"Is Father James all right?" she asked. "I haven't seen him around lately." Her voice sounded calm enough, but she looked now toward the ground and prodded at a pebble with the toe of her shoe.

"Ah, now," said Mrs. Mackinnon, "it's a good thing you mentioned him now, the poor man." She paused for an instant, as though considering the best way to go on. "A strange thing happened the other day to Miss Morag," she began. "A letter came from Fort William, the first letter she has received, you see, in her life. It was read out to her in the post office. Some cousin was dying there in Fort William—a relation of her mother's, I think it was, a spinster without a friend, you see, to turn to." She shifted the shopping basket from one arm to the other.

"Anyway, Miss Morag was so pleased with this, and never having left Kintillo since the day that she was born, she went straight up the hill to Father James and demanded some money for her fare to Fort William.

" 'I'm going,' she said. 'The cousin is dying and I'm going. I'll be back when I've nursed her decently into the grave.' And so she went—just like that, without fixing on anyone to be looking after him meantime—in her best hat and coat, with her clothes wrapped up in a wicker basket and waiting the very next morning for the ferry boat from Kyle."

Meriel looked at the ground again. She felt both hot and cold. The blood burned in her face and the rest of her body felt numb.

"So I was thinking," Mrs. Mackinnon said placidly, "myself and Mr. Mackinnon, that seeing you haven't fixed yet on a job, and besides the grand work you're doing keeping company with your father and the laird, you could go up there and give a hand to your parish priest from time to time."

When Meriel looked quickly into her face there was neither irony there nor the least suspicion.

"From time to time?" she repeated.

"Myself and Mrs. Garvie will take in his washing for the present and look after the church; and Mrs. Garvie, having less than some of us to do, can spare the time to tidy out his rooms twice a week and take up the provisions. It would be grand for the poor man if'n yourself could cook him a meal ·or two in the evenings there, when his work is done."

"Uh, huh," said Meriel.

Sometimes, for no more than a second or two, it seems as

though the bones of some reality are quickly and suddenly exposed, although this feeling never lasts and is soon forgotten. It occurred to Meriel while she stood with Mrs. Mackinnon in the road that a chain of circumstances both before her and behind had been long ago set up, and that nothing at any time had kept her from the priest.

"I'll be going," said Mrs. Mackinnon. She shifted the shopping basket from her left arm back to her right, where she always carried it.

"Certain," she said, smiling at Meriel. "You do lighten the day for your father, and for the old man too."

Meriel flushed and turned away. When she came back from her walk the sheep still lay in the same position in the road. But now its sick eyes were shut and its head was drawn further in upon its neck. When she looked at it more closely she saw that it was dead.

That evening the three of them, Meriel, her father, and Sir John, sat down to dinner together as usual.

There was vegetable soup from a tin, thickened with the same fat beads of barley and onion strips that Mrs. Mackinnon threw into every stock she cooked. Sir John spooned it noisily into his mouth, spilling a little of each mouthful down his chin. He gazed directly into the candlelight, sometimes shutting his eyes and leaning toward it as though lifting his face, by an open window, to the heat of the sun.

He had fallen from his bed onto the stone-flagged floor the morning that Anne was leaving, and though nothing was broken, the shock had affected his brain, so that some patches of his conversation made no sense at all and others were quite displaced in time.

Mrs. Mackinnon came in with three lobsters on an oval plate and put them down on the sideboard.

"Fresh, sir, this morning from Danny's boat," she said as she took away the old man's soup plate.

"Well, last summer," he said, "I remember we had two or three of these each, and the mayonnaise was fresh then, too."

"That'll be a while ago now," answered Mrs. Mackinnon. She smiled at Meriel as she passed her chair, but Meriel, remembering their conversation together in the road, refused to look up for fear of seeing in the housekeeper's eyes a sudden understanding of a different sort between them.

"We used to have proper helpings," Sir John was saying. "I remember when we would eat three or four of these lobsters at a time, and they were a good size too. I should call these things crayfish," he said, picking one up by the tail and holding it in front of him.

"Is everything satisfactory, then?" asked Mrs. Mackinnon from the doorway. "You have everything you want?"

Charles Finlay nodded. "You may go," he said. "We'll have our coffee in the study."

"It's always the same," he complained when the door had shut. "She overcooks them so that the flesh is invariably tough and tasteless."

The old man interrupted him.

"Have I told you," he said to Meriel, "about the day I swapped a packet of cigarettes for a horse?"

He had told this story many times before, but Meriel now shook her head and asked him to tell her the whole thing again, for she had forgotten exactly how it was. Charles Finlay listened with mounting annoyance as the story lengthened. He couldn't imagine how his daughter managed to look so interested and even now and then to laugh aloud.

Finlay could not abide to hear such anecdotes well told. They reminded him of an incident some twenty years earlier which still filled him with shame. As a young subaltern quartered in Stirling Castle he had heard a joke one night in the Mess which amused him enormously. He had taken care to memorize this joke, and from time to time he would look out for an opportunity to repeat it. Then, one night there had been a large dinner party at the colonel's house. The food and wines were excellent and all the guests were in high spirits. By the time the port was handed around, one or two of Finlay's brother officers had begun to tell sly army jokes at which Finlay himself, now flushed with drinking, laughed more uncontrollably than anybody. And then something terrible and unexpected took place. Finlay, without realizing any longer what he was doing, interrupted his commanding officer in the middle of a sentence and began to repeat his joke. And even worse than this, he started with the wrong end of the story first. The point at which he realized his mistake took on the nightmarish quality of slow motion. The table around him had grown silent. The other guests now avoided looking at him, and he could sense among them the same polite hostility that a newcomer feels on joining a well-organized and close-knit team. And later, when looking briefly into the colonel's face, Finlay saw a look of total contempt.

In his morbid sensitivity he could still remember each detail of the evening as though it had just taken place. For this reason he could scarcely wait until the old man was finished; he had already interrupted him briskly once or twice to correct certain facts or details in his story.

Meriel, seated between them, was eating the lobster greedily. She took lavish helpings of mayonnaise and scraped the shell with the flat of her fork until it was clean. Whenever it occurred to her, she would lean forward and help her grandfather with his food, extracting fat morsels of flesh from the claws and spooning these into his mouth. Generally, however, she forgot about him. Her thoughts would turn toward the priest, and here her heart began to beat unpleasantly, and the distance between them dissolved, so that his face was clearer to her than anything in the room around her. At such times she would feel weak and stupid with panic.

"Is it possible," Finlay said, leaning toward her across his pudding plate, "just now and then to have the luxury of a few words from you?"

Meriel flushed and began to fidget with her napkin. He found her silence offensive, and seeing for a moment how readily the blood rose to her skin, he felt the same quick pleasure that a bully feels when he has just discovered a certain weakness in his victim.

"Considering," he went on, "that you have so little to do all day—"

"I cleaned out the box room in the attic," she answered. "I found trunks of old clothes there and boxes of rubbish. There were some—"

Here she stopped, however, for she had found silk summer dresses in the attic, cloche hats with fine gauze veils, and other paraphernalia that had belonged to her mother. Now, thinking of these beautiful clothes, the faint smell of scent that still hung among the folds, and the fine silk that was scarcely worn, she felt a queer sadness in her—a feeling that was sweet and at the same time painful. Throughout the rest of the meal, and later while they drank their coffee together, she talked to her father politely about a number of things which interested neither of them. Besides this conversation, there were other thoughts in her mind, entirely unconnected with it—and these concerned her mother.

Tucked away among the drawers and cupboards about the house were certain objects—notebooks, diaries, gramophone records—that had once belonged to Mary Finlay. No one had thought to throw them away, and sometimes Meriel, opening a drawer or a dusty cupboard and finding them there, would feel a sense of shock, as though for a moment she had touched her mother's hand or heard her voice. But these

small possessions—the books, the gloves, and ornaments—
were fragments which merely gave a vague impression of the
whole. And it had only just occurred to Meriel, while
speaking of them, that these boxes of clothes completed an
extraordinary and vivid picture of her mother.

An hour later, in the dead silence of the darkened house,
Meriel crept back down the wide stairs and into the hall.
Beneath her father's bedroom door there was still the faint
light of a bedside lamp. She passed the next section of the
stairs swiftly, for this light was something she had not taken
into account. In the darkness a house takes on a new and
often frightening character. The ticking in the pipes and the
creaking of a shifting floorboard alter at night and become
menacing in subtle ways. So Meriel, who was only half
familiar with these sounds, listened fearfully to the soft
movement of the wind outside in the creepers, and to the
rattle of the landing windows.

In the hall, her slippered feet made a thin skidding sound
on the bare stone, and she paused once or twice to look
upward to the point on the landing outside her father's room.
It was not yet completely dark. The thickening twilight still
filtered through the high windows and centered on the pale
gray square of a mirror by the study door. The glass surround
of this fine Venetian mirror, weighing half a hundredweight,
was elaborately and beautifully decorated. Meriel was now
drawn toward it almost reluctantly, as though she were
afraid of what she might see there. Among the shadows of the
open hall her reflection was indistinct and its details vague
and confused. Nevertheless, she looked extraordinary. On her
head was a little cloche hat, the veil of which hung down
across her face and obscured it, so that her body in the dim
light seemed practically headless. Around her neck and
throat were several rows of jet beads that glittered queerly

and fell almost to her waist. She wore a black chiffon dress striped with broad bands of silver thread, and this too gleamed in an eerie way in the semidarkness. The dress fell in irregular folds to her knees, and on her feet she wore two grotesque little silver slippers with platform heels. The whole effect was of some mad and dissipated puppet, held up by invisible strings from crumpling in a heap to the floor.

There was nothing moving about her appearance at all. Nor did it resemble the impression of her mother which she had set out to create. Meriel at once began to giggle, and a quite extraordinary gaiety now filled her. Still moving cautiously on her platform shoes, she crossed the hall and went into the study. Here she closed the door gently and switched on the light. In a small cupboard by the fireplace she knew there were kept a number of very old gramophone records. These were all 78s that had at one time been left there by her mother. Meriel switched on the gramophone and squatted down by the cupboard on her heels to examine the records. They were cold to the touch and unexpectedly heavy. In some places the grooves were worn away; others were badly scratched. And on the labels were a number of orchestras that she had never heard of, and on one particular label was written a strange title: "The Black Bottom." Meriel had now reached a certain weakened state in which everything seemed ridiculous to her. The slightest oddity was enough to set her off on a wild fit of giggling. The simple words "Black Bottom" now struck her as being so amusing that for several seconds she laughed uncontrollably. And again when she slipped the record onto the turntable and listened to the first few bars of the music, a fresh outburst of the same wild giggling overcame her. The tune was sweet and catchy, however. The saxophone rose up in a great wide beat, and below it, like the second thread of an interlinked chain, the piano followed.

Gradually the music completed a certain mood in her that had been missing all evening. She felt calmer somehow, and her senses had loosened so that the rhythm now started to flow throughout her body. Presently she turned the record over and began to dance languidly to the tune of a slow fox trot. Her chiffon dress moved in the same gentle rhythm, and the jet beads around her neck clicked one row against another in the cleft between her breasts. In the middle of this scene, at the point where the music had reached a certain plaintive crescendo, Charles Finlay walked into the room. Over his pajamas he wore a strange-looking dressing gown, gaudily patterned in a Paisley print, and his feet were clad in Moroccan slippers with long pointed toes. It seemed to Meriel, as she stood and stared at him, that she took in these details with a startling clarity.

For several minutes there was a total silence, and in the space of this silence Meriel and her father were both suspended. Deep in the side woods a night bird called out in its flight through the woods, and the sound could be clearly heard inside the room. There were two dull spots of color on Finlay's cheeks; the rest of his face was pale. His eyes seemed to travel in a straight line from the absurd cloche hat to the silver slippers. Meriel closed her eyes and waited while her father watched her intently from the shadows by the door. In her face he could see the same mute resistance which reminded him of her mother long ago, and this resemblance was so strong that for a minute he confused them in his mind.

"You are nothing but a slut," he said distinctly.

Meriel slid off the arm of the sofa where she had sat down, and smoothed out the creases in the chiffon dress. She walked around her father toward the door, in the same lazy, unhurried way that she normally walked. She swayed her hips a little as she passed him, so that the folds of her dress brushed for a second against his legs.

She stopped for a moment in the open doorway, and Finlay now felt a sharp rush of cold air from the hall.

"Good night," she said abruptly. "When I've changed I'm going out."

15

She had nothing planned. Her calm had gone now, leaving her frightened. There was no time to imagine what she would say to the priest when he opened the door. And with the light behind him, she would lose the expression in his face, could judge nothing by it, whether to go in with him or to leave.

She turned to look back down the hill. The cold and the sea mist together were so dense they seemed made of a single solid material which caught in her throat and stifled her. The village lights were out by half past ten, and the house was hidden by the side woods in the valley. Below her the sea crept out so gently down the beach it might have frozen there in patterns to the sand.

If there was a single light down there I'd go home, she thought. And if he opened the door before I reached it, I should be caught here half up and down the hill.

The light above the door was out. The house looked deserted, and when she touched the bell the noise seemed to spring alive under her hand and to echo afterward inside her head. When Father James opened the door she was standing there staring at him, frozen and dumb. He stood in the open doorway, and the light behind him fell full on Meriel. He leaned against the side of the door with his arms folded across his chest and stared at her as though he had never seen her before in his life. He was strangely dressed in jeans and a frayed checked shirt. The sleeves of his shirt were rolled up above the elbows. There were fine blond hairs on his forearms and above the loose opening of his collar.

Meriel pulled the muffler down from her face.

"I came to see if I could help you—with the dishes and things. . . ."

The naked light bulb in the hall behind him shone directly into her eyes, and while she looked at it, this light seemed to swell and grow brighter and brighter, until the priest was nothing but a shadow between them.

"If I've come too late, I'll come back some other time—"

"No," he said slowly. "Now you're here you'd better come in out of the cold."

She followed him into the narrow hall, and while she took off her coat and the muffler from around her neck he gazed at her without any expression in his face. Meriel began to talk hurriedly.

"Is this your kitchen?" she asked, pushing open the swinging door. "What a mess. I should have come before—I only heard about Miss Morag this morning—"

"Why didn't you go back?" he asked.

She looked up at him quickly. "Did no one tell you? I decided to stay—I wanted to stay here."

Father James was hanging her coat on a peg in the hall; he turned when she spoke to him and looked at her steadily for a minute. In his eyes she imagined a total understanding, but almost immediately his face was vacant again, and sleepy, as though he were thinking of nothing at all. He looked at her body in the light through the kitchen door. Meriel wore cotton trousers and a jersey shrunken and matted from overwashing. The sleeves of this jersey were too short and the front of it dragged against her breasts. The trousers had also shrunk so that the elastic of her knickers showed plainly underneath at the waist. The priest considered all this in a slow and unfamiliar way, as though they shared a secret together which had just then been formed. The atmosphere in the room reminded Meriel of those nightmares in which her body moved weightlessly, and where each step forward left her motionless and in the same place. She went toward the sink, and Father James, leaning against the door, watched her while she stacked the dirty plates and dishes in a bowl. A piece of cold spaghetti slipped from a plate onto the draining board, and she picked it up carefully with a fork and scraped it into the dustbin underneath the sink.

"Tell me about nineteen-year-old girls," he said suddenly from the doorway. "I don't know many. I wish I had a sister of about your age. I should like to know if many young girls get dressed up in trousers as tight as those and go out at night to look after the village priest. . . ."

Meriel said nothing. She washed each plate very carefully and put it in the rack to dry. She licked the side of her cheek where a tear was sliding down toward her mouth. Father James left the doorway and came over toward the sink. Behind him the swinging door creaked shut.

"But I never realized before," he said in the same gentle voice, "how unselfish you were. When I think about it, you've given up so many things—your friends, your work, even your boyfriends (because I'm certain you do have boyfriends). And you've chosen to stay here—in this dead-end place—but now you are free, as it turns out," he added softly, "to help me here."

"I stayed here to look after them—my father and grandfather—to keep them company."

"I see."

"Besides, I hated Edinburgh," she said in a whisper. The plates were now washed up and she turned to the cutlery.

"So you did—I was forgetting that."

He picked up a dishcloth from the side of the sink and one of the plates from the drying rack.

"Would you like me to help you?" he asked. "It's a good thing you came, really. I'm very grateful. Mrs. Garvie has had flu for the last two days. But I expect you knew that already."

Meriel shook her head. The tears were falling down her face so fast she could no longer see what she was doing, and the knives and forks had begun to swell monstrously in the bowl and to slip about in her hands. She thought that if he would only move—even a foot or two to the side—she would be able to get to the door, but he was standing so close behind her that she could feel the heat of his body through his clothes. While she was thinking this, that she would never speak to him again, or walk up the road to hear Mass in his church, or eat again at the same table so long as he was dining there, the priest said suddenly in a different tone of voice: "Are you crying? Don't cry—please don't cry."

He put his hands on her shoulders and pulled her around in such a way that she fell against his chest. While she cried there for a little, noisily and without control, he stroked her hair and patted her gently on the back. "Don't cry," he repeated over and over again. "Don't cry." The matted wool of her jersey clung to her skin, and suddenly the priest sighed and pushed her away from him.

"Come and sit down," he said. "I'll make you a strong cup of coffee—the way Magnus makes it." He spoke to her now as though she were a child, leading her toward the table and pushing her gently down into a chair. He went to the sink and filled a kettle, and while it came to the boil he watched her intently until her shoulders had stopped shaking and she sat quietly at the table. Then he left her and went to the cupboard under the stairs where the drink was kept and brought back a bottle of whisky, slipping a little into two mugs and setting them down on a corner of the table. Meriel watched him listlessly. Now and then she gave a deep sigh, all that was left of her storm of crying.

He sat down and pushed a mug toward her. "Come on, drink it," he said. "It will do you good."

She ignored him. Though it no longer mattered, she was wondering how much of her mascara had washed down around her cheeks and mouth. She made a triangle in the crook of her hand with some crumbs that were on the table.

"Listen to me—" he began.

She wondered what kind of fool he must take her for, since there was nothing he could say that would soften her.

"I have to go now—" she said politely.

"Wait till I've said what I have to say, and then you can go. I have the only job in the world," he went on, "where if I—where if you stay here tonight with me—I can't get up in the morning and go on with."

His hands were clasped so tightly around his mug that they were red and must have burned from the heat inside it. He was sitting there very quietly as though he had only that moment understood what he was saying, and Meriel felt a sudden intense pity for him. This feeling was both violent and fragile, and its strength astonished her. She put out a hand and touched him lightly on the arm.

"I wish—" she began.

She would have liked to explain it to him—this and other things besides, that now seemed suddenly quite clear to her, but the priest had sprung to his feet and started to walk rapidly up and down the room.

He told Meriel to go home—that he found her beautiful and even desirable, and wasn't this enough for her?—that if only she would go home she might think of him alone there and miserable without her. He said that it was time he fetched her coat and took her back, and yet, on his way to the door, he changed his mind. He turned sharply before he reached it and went on walking up and down the same stretch of floor between the table and the sink.

Meriel watched him placidly, sitting sideways in the chair. She was no longer afraid of him or of anything they might do together. She heard the tap dripping in the sink, and beyond it the sound of a sudden wind that was lifting along the shoulder of the hill and moaning between the window frames. These things appeared to her like the first signs of the storm into which she was walking as she went with light steps toward the priest.

This storm seemed to lift them both from separate corners of the room toward each other, and at its center there was a sudden blindness.

When he had taken her up the stairs, however, and had closed the door of his room, the priest turned away from Meriel and would not look at her. Beneath her bare feet she felt the cold of the lino floor. For the rest, she felt nothing beyond the simplest emotions—a strong desire for him and a certain boldness. She began to undress calmly and without hurrying. She pulled the jersey over her head and later the shirt, in such a way that her breasts, once freed, lifted in a single pure movement beneath her upraised arms. And afterward she shook out her hair so that it fell in a mass about her shoulders. All this she did with a certain easy grace of which she was totally aware.

The priest, from his position by the door, now turned and gazed at her naked body. He looked at it in the same grave way that he might have considered a long-awaited present, delivered to him and duly unwrapped. He put out his hand and stroked the skin of her arms and breasts in a slow deliberate way, and then, as though a certain tension were now released in him, he pulled her body toward him and began to make love to her.

There was a certain shape to the time that followed. Just as the last daylight gave way to the cold beams of the rising moon, and in the same slow fashion returned, so the night between Meriel Finlay and the priest passed through three particular stages. For some time they made love and were aware of nothing in the room around them; later they talked for a while, and again they made love.

Violent lovemaking, like the two acts of birth and death, takes place in an almost total darkness, so that afterward these sensations are inexpressible and only certain details remain. The angle of a hand against the window, the taste of salt on the skin: these details are vivid and confused.

And there is finally the bewildering sense that the body, from a single firm place, is pitched into an open and steadily falling darkness. All these images afterward passed through Meriel's brain like scenes formed quickly on a darkened screen. They were without sequence or even a fixed place in time.

Presently, while they lay quietly together in the bed, she looked around the room. She took in the narrow cupboard, the faint pattern of the shabby curtains, and the exact slant of the moonlight across the open floor. It seemed to her that by fixing such simple details in her mind she would come to terms with her own astonishing happiness. But having said to herself, this is how it is, the bed here, the clothes in a heap beside it, the table over there and the bedside lamp, her sense of unreality remained. The room was cut off from her normal life. She could neither imagine it now in the daylight nor the priest alone there again without her.

He leaned on one elbow on the pillow, and the bed was so narrow that half of his weight was resting against her. He played with her hair, combing his fingers through it and arranging it in such a way that it spread out like threads of a loosely woven material against the pillow. The moonlight had drained the room of color. The pillow was a startling white, and her hair laid out across it was black and without luster.

"I noticed your hair," he said; "first your hair, and then your body." He paused and smiled at her. "And later your face."

"In that order?"

"In that order."

She smiled back at him.

"And do you still?"

"No," he said simply. "Now you are all of one piece to me."

He lay down again in the bed and closed his eyes.

"The other night," he said, "I sat down to write to you. I was lonely. I started to write you this letter. . . ."

Here he stopped. And when she asked him what it was he had written, he told her there had been nothing, nothing of any importance, and later he had torn up the letter.

She ran one hand across his body. The skin was damp, for he had made love to her with a strange intensity, and she could feel the speed at which his heart still beat.

"Listen—" she began.

She was filled with a sudden tenderness toward him. This tenderness was deep and heavy, and though she searched for them she could find no words to express it. Nor did he listen. He stroked her hair away from her face and lightly kissed her in the hollow of the neck where the skin was warm and the pulse beat strongly beneath. He did not refer again to the past. They made no plans to meet again, and they behaved as though a time beyond the limits of the room did not exist.

In this strange state, almost nothing disturbed them. From

time to time they listened to the sound of the wind outside in the night, and through the window they watched the progress of the moon. Meriel looked up at one time and saw it suspended from the middle of a single pane, so fierce a light that the stars around it were almost invisible. But later when she looked again the moon had gone and the sky was almost light.

It was five o'clock in the morning when the priest took Meriel home down the road. Across the sky, driven by a high wind, thin shreds of cloud passed over the moon, and the same wind rattled in the trees and slammed at the rectory gate. The sea came in at a southwest slant across the sound, and the full path of the gale struck a corner of the bay as they were coming down the hill. The priest had an arm around Meriel's shoulders. Long strands of her hair worked loose from her headscarf and whipped against his cheek.

"Let's run," she said. "Come on, let's run down the rest of the way."

He couldn't hear her, for he sheltered her, and the warm wind drummed in his ears. When they came to the bridge, he stopped there and pulled her back against the parapet.

"I have to leave you here," he said. "Will you be all right?"

He unbuttoned her coat and slipped his arms around her waist. He tasted the salt on her skin and in her hair. Below them the river beat against the arches of the bridge and the spray flew up across the road.

"I have to go," he said again.

Meriel stretched up and put her arms around his neck. It was neither the same night she had stood on the rectory doorstep, nor the same place. Between the two occasions she had gone through a great span of time. She asked him no questions. She was concerned with nothing beyond the next few minutes—in the face of such happiness it seemed impossible that she should put one foot in front of the other and walk away. But the priest had begun to loosen her arms from around his neck, and at the same time to distract her from what he was doing by stroking her face and kissing her. Presently he asked when the next caillie took place in the village. Meriel did not immediately see the sense of this. She was startled.

"On Saturday night," she answered. "Why? Shall you come?"

He smiled at her. "Why? Would they have me?"

She shook her head. "You can meet me afterward. You can meet me here."

"No, not here," he said after a minute. "Out in the side woods."

"By the wooden bridge."

"Yes—there, then. On Saturday night. Now you must go."

She kissed him once on the mouth and released him. He watched her running away toward the wall of the park. She ran with erratic energy, like a happy child, and her coat flapped loosely behind her in the wind. She waved to him from the top of the wall, and then she slipped down on the farther side and was out of sight.

When she had gone, Father James did not immediately turn and go back up the hill to the rectory. Some time ago in the course of the night he had reached a decision, and this decision had come to him in an odd manner. It had appeared to him fully formed and with a certain air of menace, as though a third person in the room had spoken the words aloud. And now this feeling of menace was accentuated by the queer half-light of the dawn and by the raging wind. In this unnatural light was the same effect that is found in the last thin rays of sun before the clouds of a coming storm, and the wild movement of the trees was scarcely separated from the darkness of the hills behind.

Father James now turned, and scarcely realizing what he was doing, he walked down toward the beach with his face turned full into the path of the wind. For a few minutes he stood looking out to sea. The tide was coming in and the waves formed a wide straight line like a wall across the mouth of the bay.

"I'm leaving," he said aloud, and having spoken these words he felt a sudden extraordinary weakness. The beauty of the sea in front of him and the happiness he was giving up were now confused in his mind: so that Meriel Finlay and the country he was leaving became the two parts of a single terrible loss.

When he turned to go back up the hill, the morning light was already visible above the high ridges of the Torridon hills. Behind him as he walked up the road, the first sounds of the village morning carried past him in the wind.

16

On a Saturday night, the last week in September, Meriel went to the caillie with her father.

When the laird was young and the village hall was newly built, there had been a caillie once a month, and a band to play the reels. And young girls from as far away as Inverness had won prizes there for the sword dance and the eightsome reel.

But that was more than fifty years ago, and in the time between, the caillies had become smaller, dingier affairs. Now, when the beat of the music reached a certain pitch the paper decorations descended on the heads of the dancers, and when the liquor ran out the village people went home instead of staying to sing as they used to until the morning came.

At one time an element had crept into these gatherings that was foreign and destructive. For several summers in a row, a gang of youths had come over the pass from the council houses of Strathcarron. They swaggered on the dance floor in their dirty jeans, ran pocket combs through their hair in front of the local girls, and sneered at the boys dressed up in kilts. There was one, Jim Garvie, whose hair was greasier and whose jacket was heavier with studs than all the rest, and he was the leader of this gang. He taught the girls how to jive to the music of the eightsome reel. He snapped his fingers and shook his hips and danced alone in the middle of the floor. One night while there was singing in the hall, Jim

Garvie took a young girl out among the dock leaves and the long grass at the back of the hall and made her pregnant. In those days which are now history, he was made to marry the girl by her father and two friends. They took him out again to the same long grass at the back of the hall, and they beat him until he was senseless; the rise and fall of the singing through the open windows covered every cry of protest. Now this gang no longer came in the summertime and the caillies were peaceful again, and yet there was a certain small fraction of the village who missed the air of tension that the greasers had taken away with them.

Meriel and her father went on foot to the caillie.

"It will reek," Finlay said, "of whisky and cheap tobacco in the hall. We shall need all the fresh air we can get on the way home."

They walked down the drive and along the beach road in silence. It had rained all day and a mist rose up knee-high from the ground. Several times Meriel, in her galoshes, walked into puddles, and the mud spattered up around her legs and the hemline of her dress.

"You should have worn gumboots," Finlay said.

Once a year he dressed up like a fool in full-dress tartan and he went to the caillie, as his father had done before him, and his grandfather before that. He wore the same lace jabot handed down, and the same velvet jacket with square silver buttons on the front and sleeves.

It was a beautiful night after a hard day's rain. There was a hush in the air on which the music of the caillie stretched out faint and thin like a strange lament. Alone, Charles Finlay might have walked, on his way, down to the water's edge while the tide was out, across the paths of the river mouth which he knew so well that he could cross the sand on the darkest night without once wetting his feet. A gentle wind came in across the water and he lifted his face toward it as a blind man might turn his eyes toward the heat of the sun. All this time he was conscious of Meriel walking silently beside him, and of his dullness, which cut him off from her and made him seem ugly. As they walked up the steps of the village hall, he took one long deep breath of the night air before he followed her through the door.

There was an eightsome reel in progress. The windows of the hall were entirely steamed up and the bare wood boards shook to the pounding of the music. It took some time for the village people to notice that the laird's son had arrived. In those few minutes Finlay wore the cold expression of someone who had a disagreeable duty to perform and intended to get through it as quickly as possible.

When the music stopped, however, and the floor began to clear, something humiliating took place which he had neither remembered nor envisaged. Little by little the talking and the laughter died away. One face after another was turned toward the doorway. Small groups of people close to him broke up and flattened themselves against the wall. And they were not looking at his pretty daughter, who was only waiting to be noticed and asked to dance. The entire hall was focused like a great collective eye on Finlay himself, and this eye neither approved nor condemned, but seemed to isolate them both and pin them back against the wall. The silence lasted for perhaps thirty seconds, but by this time Meriel looked ready to cry and Finlay was conscious of a fine cold sweat on his hands and forehead.

The factor now came forward a little too eagerly and stumbled against a chair leg as he approached. He wore a fixed look of gaiety. This look, put on at the entrance to the hall, was the same that he wore on every similar occasion. Beside him his wife began to speak about several different things at once. While she was shaking hands with him she admired Finlay's lace jabot, the nice playing of the three-piece band, and Meriel's pretty dress, in the same rushed sentence.

Meriel, like her father, now wore an expression of proud indifference, and when they were taken to their seats against the wall she settled herself on the edge of the chair and stared mulishly in front of her. The factor Jefferson and his wife sat down beside them.

Jefferson had a certain working relationship with his employer and one on which he prided himself. It was a delicate balance between his superior knowledge and training on the one hand and Finlay's authority on the other. So long as they were both confined by the farm office walls or within the grounds of the estate, this balance was maintained. But directly they met socially, Jefferson gave way to an almost uncontrollable panic. He could think of nothing whatsoever to say. Even worse than this, his wife chattered on in a gushing way that humiliated him. He now sat beside his employer, rubbing his hands violently together, and he could hardly screw up five decent words into a sentence.

The music started up again. It was a fox trot that no one had played south of the border in the past ten years. Danny the lobsterman's two daughters walked out onto the floor and began to dance languorously together, neither one looking the other in the face, or speaking. Presently, a young shepherd selected the fattest girl in the room and danced with her in a curious swooping movement, as though he were trying to lift her and carry her bodily across the room. Gradually the floor filled up. But the dancers, in the main, were middle-aged, and most of the younger men stood around the bar at one end of the hall. They stood there awkwardly, as if their bodies were better suited to the swaying of a boat or their feet to the mud of plowed fields.

The very old men sat silently, smoking and drinking. When they looked at the dance floor at all, they stared with complete indifference at the couples moving around it.

Presently the factor, seeing an opportunity to escape, blew his nose noisily once or twice and stood up to ask Meriel Finlay for a dance. Meriel, who had been staring moodily at the band a moment before, now rose in a swift graceful movement and gave the factor her arm. Finlay, glancing just then in her direction, surprised on her face a look of sudden gaiety, as though the atmosphere of the evening had changed from one moment to the next and, from being intolerably dull, was now filled with promise.

Charles Finlay was now alone. The two seats on either side of him were empty. He had two alternatives: to remain where he was until Meriel returned, or to walk back toward the entrance where a gathering was centered around the bar. The second of these two he did not consider, for he was never at ease with his subordinates. He was a man they preferred to visit together in twos or threes. While they were with him they were careful to speak in generalities; he would feel in them a simple animal antagonism which further increased his own reserve. So now he would not go up and drink with his tenants at the bar or pretend, besides, a camaraderie which he did not feel.

In the course of the evening Finlay danced once with his daughter, a foursome reel, and later a waltz with his housekeeper, Mrs. Mackinnon. Finlay was a fine dancer and a good-looking man. His back was straight and his feet were both neat and self-assured. From time to time, as he danced, a brief look of pleasure would cross his face, but this look was gone again almost the instant he sat down.

One thing, however, brightened the long and tedious evening. Meriel, in the last two hours, had scarcely once sat down to rest. She danced every dance with a different partner, and there was an extraordinary radiance in her which her father had never seen before. Gradually, Finlay became aware that she was the center of attention. Whenever she stood up to dance, there was an imperceptible tightening in the atmosphere. The crowd at the bar would shift and regroup in such a way that they could get a better look at the dance floor. And each of her partners in turn seemed to sense a special warmth in her, to which they responded. Now the competition was not fierce. With the exception of Meriel, there were scarcely two women in the hall with passable good looks. Nevertheless, Charles Finlay felt an intense pride of ownership and of achievement, and wherever she was in the room his eyes repeatedly strayed toward her. At such times his whole face would soften and his body would briefly relax.

When Meriel sat down at last beside him, she was flushed from the heat in the room, and her arms and shoulders drooped with exhaustion. She turned to smile at him. And this smile indicated that she was exceptionally happy, that she was finding the whole evening delightful and loved everyone around her.

"Wait," she said, catching hold of his arm. "In a minute now Danny will begin to sing."

But when he started to answer, Meriel had already turned away from him and was waving to someone across the hall.

The three musicians were drinking neat whisky, and their accordions lay on the floor at their feet. There was a sense of general unrest in the hall, and in that sudden quiet after the shouting and stamping of the reels there was nothing whatsoever to do.

There comes a time, at a good caillie, when just so much is drunk, and out of this a certain mood builds up a sweet regret for times past and finished with. Then after a while, softly, and almost for himself alone, someone will start singing. Three people in the village could sing in such a way that a person listening to them would feel a chill run along the length of his spine and a certain emotion rise up in him that was gentle and bitter. One of these singers was Mary Lee Macdonald.

Sometimes the first few notes she sang were hesitant, and at other times her voice rose up easily and clearly from the silence. Sometimes she sang alone for as much as half an hour, and at other times the lobsterman sang with her, and the songs they sang were almost always sad.

They have memories there that go back beyond their lives to a time when the living was easier and the land was rich with cattle and good crops. Mary Lee and the lobsterman would sing of the years before the sheep destroyed these lands. They would sing, too, some nights, of the islands that are out of reach across the waters and of long journeys which ended in loneliness and death.

Mary Lee sang alone that night, the song of the Whirlpool Corievrechan and the great tide races of Camuslang and the same waters of the Minch in which her husband, a lobsterman, had drowned five years before.

While she was singing Charles Finlay felt something rise up in his chest that sickened him. His throat was constricted, and at the same time the rest of his body felt weak and fluid. Blindly he turned from the singer's face and fixed his eyes on an empty corner of the room. But presently his mood settled again and he began without thinking to bite his nails.

When Mary Lee stopped singing it was past midnight, and for a while no one spoke. Then gradually the village people began to shift about on the hard-backed chairs, and the dreaming slipped out of their faces. They waited for the laird's son to leave.

17

They had been standing for some time now, Meriel and the priest, among the trees that bordered the river. Leaning against the thick trunk of an oak, their bodies left on the ground a single shadow that was sometimes detached from the tree and sometimes melted into it. For a long time they scarcely spoke, and the priest, with his eyes closed, stroked Meriel softly and lazily beneath her coat, and with his mouth he explored the skin of her neck and face.

Meriel had this effect on him; directly he had seen her coming toward him, a pale slight figure in the darkness of the woods, he had forgotten entirely the reason for their meeting. And now when he loosened his hold on her and looked down into her face, it was impossible to speak to her of the things that were in his mind.

Father James was a gentle man. He had a fear both of hurting and of being hurt. Once as a child he had witnessed a fierce argument between his parents. He had stayed in the room out of a simple terror that their anger, like an undirected wind, would veer suddenly toward him if he moved. The argument had leaped from one subject to another, continually finding fresh aspects on which to feed itself. And finally his mother, with a cry of distress, had run from the room with her hands over her face. It had seemed to him at the time that something senseless and cruel had taken place. He could not forget it.

Meriel's face was now upturned toward him. Even in the

half-light he could see her happiness. It now seemed brutal to destroy this happiness so soon after meeting her.

"Tell me about the caillie," he said softly.

"The caillie," she answered, "well, it was like this—"

She too seemed distracted, however, and did not complete the sentence. Her movements were drowsy and slow. With one finger she brushed his eyelids, and then his mouth.

"I danced with the lobsterman," she said presently, "the lobsterman Danny. I wish you could see him. And then later," she added, as though remembering events which had taken place some years ago, "later, they began to sing, and the singing was really beautiful."

"Is there only one lobsterman?"

"Only one—it doesn't pay."

A bright moon was rising over the bay, lighting up the open fields and the fringes of the wood with a strange greenish light. It cast shadows so faint across the valley that they were like patches of darker earth on the pale ground.

Over the priest's shoulder Meriel gazed out across the field. This look at first was wide and vague, and then her attention sharpened.

Something had moved in the flat silver light of the open valley.

"Look," she said quickly, "someone's there—"

The priest straightened up and turned around.

"I thought I saw someone there—by the road," she repeated.

In the moonlight, however, the road was indistinct. He could see nothing beyond a thin black line of trees that ran along the farther wall.

He leaned back against the tree. This interruption had startled him and brought him to his senses. In a short time he was leaving her. A temporary post in the Salford diocese had been found for him by his cousin. The place and the date were already fixed, and yet he had told her nothing. His heart began to beat at an increased speed.

"Meriel," he said quickly, "listen to me."

Meriel smiled and shook her head. She took his face in her hands and began to kiss him on the mouth with small and rapid kisses. But a moment later, something in his manner, or perhaps in the tone of his voice, disturbed her. Suddenly she cried out, "Ah, don't—don't speak—don't say anything."

Father James gave in to her without resistance. He pulled her around toward the tree and pressed his body against her. At the thought of leaving her a furious rebellion now overcame him. With increasing passion and confusion, he now spoke to her of many things which he had no right to mention, and he made her certain promises, too, which he would not keep.

The two people in the wood were not alone. Below a dry stone wall separating the wood from the open fields, a figure crouched among the shadows and silently listened to them. The night was very still. The air seemed liquid under the moon, and all the sounds in it were softened. At times the two voices were audible, but at others they sank to a slow murmur. And this murmuring became confused with the steady movement of the river through the trees beyond.

Miss Morag had been crouching for some time against the rough stone wall. Corn stubble pressed sharply through the cloth of her coat and into the flesh of her stockinged legs. Besides this, she was cramped from sitting doubled up in one position, and her coat was damp from the raw ground. She scarcely noticed these things, however, for a peculiar exhilaration filled her. Her heart beat so loudly she was frightened of the noise and pressed her arms across her chest to stifle it. For a while she was content to remain with her head below the level of the wall and merely to eavesdrop. For she was also afraid of the moon's strength. It shone directly across the top of the wall and with a queer intensity. Presently the two voices became increasingly hard for her to hear and Miss Morag became restless.

Little by little and with infinite patience she raised her head above the wall so that her eyes were on a level with the topmost stones. And here, not ten feet away from her, was a sight that made the housekeeper stop her breath. Among the last trees of the wood, and clearly visible against the broad trunk of an oak, the figures of Meriel Finlay and the young priest were deeply embraced. But it was not this which filled her with a sudden and unexpected heat. It was the stance of their two bodies against the tree—for the priest, with his back to her now, moved in a steady and vigorous rhythm against the young girl's body. In the same rough manner, she now remembered, as the farm bulls would rut in the open sunlight of the fields.

Her breath came in short gasps and her knees below the level of the wall were shaking. Her eyes became fixed in a dark sweet craving on the priest, and when he cried out at last as though in pain, his cry seemed to flow out from the depths of her own body. She clung to the top of the wall to prevent herself from falling down beside it, but the violence of her excitement was now too great for her, and she sank down again among the shadows, shivering and suddenly confused. She lay there, almost supine, until the last bewildering sounds had ceased and the silence of the night had returned. Above her, the moon, split up by the blunt stubble of the corn, continued to shine indifferently on her upturned face.

18

Miss Morag's memory was childlike and underdeveloped. By the following morning she had entirely forgotten her own strange behavior and thought only of the incident between Meriel Finlay and the priest. This scene took place in her mind in black and white, and its details had the sharply focused clarity of a photograph. She now had enough evidence stored up against Father James to have him hounded from Kintillo.

For a long time she had spied on him. At first these activities had given her a new interest in life, and for a while she had been certain his downfall was close at hand. But nothing had happened. Nothing of any interest whatsoever. And the waiting had become a burden. It weighed on her mind as soon as she woke up and would afterward remain with her throughout the day.

Besides this, she would feel a sense of loss which was hard to locate; and this feeling had been with her ever since she returned from visiting her cousin in Fort William. The day she had walked onto the ferry and felt the solid ground slip away from under her feet, she had been more frightened than at any other time in her life. Across the water, while she held tightly to the ferry rail, she had seen, approaching slowly through the mist, other hills like those she had left behind, and other great boats, similar to those she had seen in the Sound, pass close at hand. But from the minute that she stepped down from the ferry's decks onto dry land, she had walked into a nightmare. The din of the cars and great lorries roaring night and day through the town, the innumerable people running through the streets, the sick, frightened eyes of her cousin, had pinned her dumbly to the ground and prevented her from thinking of anything then but a place where she might hide. Mercifully, her cousin had died within the week, and Morag had found her way home again, slowly and with infinite difficulty, until she stood at last dumfounded on Kintillo pier.

Since then she had lost something irretrievable, though what it was and even how she had lost it she no longer knew. But now, as she went about her work there was a slump to her shoulders, and the spring had gone out of her walk, so that she resembled more than ever an old horse put out to graze which senses in the wind the knacker's yard.

That morning, however, things were vastly different. She was out of bed with a sharp agility. She neither looked back with regret at the bed she was leaving nor paused while she dressed to glance at the weather from her bedroom window.

In other ways which were also negative, Morag's later behavior was equally astonishing. While she served the priest his breakfast she betrayed no emotion whatsoever. She remained quite calm and under control. If her color was a little heightened, it was due to a certain plan which she had now formed carefully in her mind.

When her work in the rectory was done, the beds made and the washing up scrupulously dried and put away, Morag took her army coat from a hook by the kitchen door and went out into the raw cold air of the autumn morning.

The village shop was crowded. Since no one turned to greet her or paid her the slightest attention, Miss Morag smiled suddenly, a wide triumphant smile, and sat down in a chair by the counter to wait. When she thought of the priest again, a joy so wild and terrible flooded through her body that for a moment she felt giddy. She shut her eyes and placed one hand on the countertop to support herself.

When she opened her eyes again the shop was empty, and Jean Macpherson had closed the post office grille.

"If'n you're planning on settling here for the morning," she said, "I have work to do and you will be very much in the way."

"Just a minute," said Morag, getting up from the chair. "Just a wee minute," she said again in a wheedling voice. It was all she could do to keep herself from laughing aloud.

The postmistress ignored her. She had two heavy bags of mail beside her on the floor. While she was cutting the string from one of these she said over her shoulder, "You should know better. Nobody comes in here while I'm sorting the mail—the shop is shut.

"Shut," she repeated. She slammed a thick pile of letters down on the countertop behind the grille.

Another wave of laughter surged up in Miss Morag's throat, so that when she opened her mouth to speak she began to giggle uncontrollably. Presently she felt weak and sat down again on the chair to rest.

"I have seen them together," she said calmly, "the priest and Meriel Finlay."

She watched Jeanie's face. There was nothing there to indicate that she had heard. There was no check in the speed at which she worked. She was sorting letters into piles, and around each pile she fixed a rubber band.

"I've seen them," Miss Morag repeated, "as clear as day, hugging and kissing together—down by the wooden bridge across the river."

Without warning Jeanie Macpherson pushed open the grille between them and leaned forward. Her face was barely a few inches away from her.

"People say your mother died of syphilis," she said,

separating each word clearly from the next. "They say that's the reason you're a loonie. I say things are different. I say some are born unfortunate but others are just born wicked. I say you are crazy eaten up with envy and you always were. Since you were a child, it's those with two eyes the same, normal faces and normal ways, that drove you mad. Now, I've seen what's been going on—don't you worry. When Father James came to this parish, and him such a handsome man with fine blue eyes—you couldn't wait, you wicked old bitch, till you had him driven out again."

Throughout this speech and even when the postmistress had finished, Miss Morag stood by the counter, blinking, as though she had taken in nothing. She shut one eye slowly, and then she opened it again and shut the other.

"Now, get out," said Jeanie furiously. She shut the grille again with a snap. "Now get out of here!"

Miss Morag shook her head. Forgetting her shopping bag and even the food she had come to buy, she turned slowly around and went toward the door. The post office doors were double and one of these was on the latch. In the narrow opening she caught one hip squarely against it and gave a small whimper of pain.

When she was some way down the street, Jeanie Macpherson came out of the village shop and tossed her shopping bag into the middle of the road. Miss Morag turned her back on it and gazed down toward the beach. The tide was going out and the beach was empty. She walked on for about a hundred yards and stopped by the wall to rest. It confused her when people spoke to her too fast. Like a child, she picked out certain words, and turning these over in her mind, she forgot the rest entirely. One single insult, however, had struck her so forcibly that it was like a blow in the stomach. She sucked in her breath and leaned back against the wall. Jeanie Macpherson and the priest had the same blue eyes that were not merely blue, but of a deep unfaded blue without a flaw. It was this sense of loss, before quite inexpressible, that had haunted her ever since the day when she had first seen her reflection in a mirror.

She stayed by the wall for some time. She noticed nothing around her beyond the one thin branch of an elder bush that the wind shook violently in front of her. And when, at last, she straightened up and began to walk slowly along the road, she glanced back once at this elder bush as though it were now forever connected in her mind with the blue eyes of the priest.

When Morag had gone, the postmistress had some minutes of peace to herself. But instead of continuing with her work, she stood motionless with her hands curled loosely on the countertop and her head bowed. Presently a tear fell onto the counter, and when she had wiped it away, another fell in its place.

The doctor startled her. He came out of the sitting room so quietly that she noticed nothing until he spoke.

"What is it?" he asked. "What is it, Jeanie?"

The postmistress began to work again, more busily than before. There was an obstinate set to her face, and small traces of her former anger could be seen in the way she slammed the mail down on the counter and stamped it.

"What is it, Jeanie?" the doctor repeated.

He was comparatively sober, and his words had a sudden authority. After a pause she answered him.

"It was just Morag," she said, in a voice he could scarcely hear, "with some wild notion or other that she had in her head."

"Concerning the priest?" Magnus asked thoughtfully.

Jeanie ignored him.

"I cannot abide the woman," she continued. "Her maundering ways, the mischief that's in her, the loonie voice—"

Magnus was silent for a moment. Throughout the last two hours he had been sitting in the parlor next door. He spent an increasing amount of time there, lulled by the warmth of the paraffin stove and the sounds of the shop next door. That morning he had heard through the door brief snatches of a row between the two women, and now there was a certain hunger in him to hear the rest of it.

"What notion was this?" he asked. "What story?"

Jeanie shook her head. The mail was sorted at last. There was nothing for her to do—there were no customers to serve and nothing on the counter that needed rearranging. She turned her gaze to the window and out across the bay. A low mist had come down over the valley. The landscape was flat and dreary and the trees above the shore stood out, a dull gray against the hill behind.

Magnus was now considering the best way to go on. The Highlander is secretive. His loyalties, by reason of his isolated life, are deep and sometimes inexplicable. Thus, for some reason, Jeanie Macpherson defended the priest, although from whom or from what he could not discover. (It did not occur to him that the postmistress feared the effects of his tongue in much the same way that she feared Miss Morag.)

He pulled up a chair. It was the same chair on which Morag had sat a while before, and he leaned his elbows on the counter. When he was sober the doctor had both charm and persuasion. He used these two weapons with gentle cunning on the girl in front of him.

"Listen to me now," he said softly. "How long have I known you, Jeanie? How many years is it you have been a solace to me in my loneliness and affliction?"

In spite of herself, the postmistress smiled.

"About ten years, I should say," she replied.

"Ten years, is it?" He seemed surprised at this. "Ten years

. . . that's a grand length of time now. And in that time," he went on, "I have never seen you cry. Not under the worst conditions. Not once. And bearing in mind the husband you have, the children and so forth—" he added briskly. "But this story of the priest—and it does concern him, doesn't it?—now why should it make you cry?"

"Ah, it was nothing, Doctor," she answered placidly. "Nothing at all when I think of it."

Magnus studied her in the same shrewd way that he might have studied the vagaries of a former patient. There were many kinds of lying, half-truths, distortions, and he had heard most of them. This last, however, took the biscuit. It certainly took some beating in its simplicity.

"Amongst friends," he went on patiently, "there is such a thing as the courtesy of the truth. A politeness, wouldn't you say, that is somehow due between them."

"Well, now," she answered in the same placid voice, "the truth is many things, Doctor." She went over to the window and leaned against the sill. "If the truth were just the one thing, just what you saw now, then we would all be beggars, wouldn't we?"

At this moment a little bell rang above the shop door, and Mrs. Garvie, a widow from down the street, came in for her morning groceries. She greeted the doctor warmly and started at once to give him the details of her ailments, chilblains and so forth, that she had just then remembered. And afterward when she spoke to Jeanie, her list of groceries was of the same order, an ounce of this, a quarter of that, a few penceworth of the other.

With some effort the doctor prevented himself from groaning aloud. He leaned heavily on the countertop and began to bite his nails. Mrs. Garvie was there for several minutes, and when she had gone the silence resumed. But it was now of a different order. There was a certain tension in it, for Jeanie had made up her mind to something. She now gave the doctor a look which was swift, subtle, and charged with inferences.

"Since you'll hear it from other sources," she began, "I'll tell you the story myself. For all," she added, "it's not worth repeating."

Magnus let out his breath in a long slow sigh. He said nothing.

"Aye, it's about the priest," she said quietly. "Morag has been spying on him for a time past now. She has it fixed in her head that he's carrying on with some affair."

"With what affair?" he asked in a whisper. "With whom?" But he knew quite well who it was before she answered. An ice-cold sickness filled him. For an instant, too, he could not breathe. There was a retching sound in his throat, and the postmistress leaned forward and gazed at him in alarm.

"Are you all right?" she asked.

Magnus straightened himself on the counter.

"Well, go on," he said impatiently. "Go on, go on, finish it, for God's sake."

"That's all there's to it. A storm in a teacup. Fancies that she has in her maggoty head. Maybe some trick of the light, the trees moving there down by the bridge." But she had said too much and was now ashamed of herself. "The priest is a good and honest man," she said quickly, "no matter what he does now."

Fortunately the doctor was no longer listening. He sat slumped against the counter. After his sudden shock he felt weary and cold. Later he would feel a hatred for the priest which would astound him. But now he stared in a mild, almost bovine way at the postmistress; when he got up from the chair his movements were disconnected, as though he had suffered, in the last few minutes, some form of stroke.

By the counter Jeanie called after him softly.

"If'n there's truth in such a story," she said, "it won't all of it be found—and besides, there are none of us here who will want to know it."

Before leaving, Magnus turned to say good-bye. Against the dark wall behind her and the rows of boxes on the jumbled shelves, her face appeared white and dim. She looked about as real to him as a small wax doll propped up on the countertop.

In the same state of unreality, he wandered home along the road. He had forgotten his car in the village street and it remained there for the night. All forewarnings, premonitions, and such were of no use to him. In a brief span of time he had followed this simple story through to a certain ending. He could see that one day the priest and Meriel Finlay would leave together. They might marry perhaps. But this did not concern him. In any event he would remain alone. As he walked down the road, the puddles in the ruts shone faintly in the sky's reflection. Magnus noticed these and other things in the same way that a sick man, returning slowly to consciousness, fixes his eyes on totally meaningless objects.

From time to time a sudden dizziness came back to him and he staggered slightly on the muddy surface of the road. To the passersby, when their greetings went unanswered, he resembled the drunken parody of himself that they had often seen going home when the pubs had closed.

Alone on the road, when he had passed the last house between the villages, Magnus sat down on the damp verge by the edge of the road and began to weep.

"Ah, Meriel," he said over and over agan. "Ah, my little Meriel."

The words brought him a strange comfort. Indeed the very sounds of his grief began to drown the sense of it, so that presently he blew his nose loudly and rose to his feet. The hill was steep, and Magnus cursed bitterly from time to time as he struggled up the muddy path—the gradient seemed sharper, somehow, and there were boulders in his way that had not been there before. Halfway up the slope he stopped for a while to rest. Out in the bay, between the clouds, the sun came down in narrow strips across the water, and beyond, toward the sound, patches of the same light flickered on the open sea. It was a view which Meriel had loved. She used to sit by herself sometimes, on the bench outside, watching the sun go down. "Ah, Magnus," she had said to him once, "if I had this view when I was old—" The doctor thought of her now in the past tense, and a dissipated sweetness, for an instant, crossed his face.

"For I have loved her," he crooned to himself, "throughout the long days—and most of them alone."

Later, when he was seated at last in a chair by the empty grate, he amended this statement to himself aloud.

"Not loved her," he said simply, "but lusted after her."

Presently he fell asleep in the chair with his head resting on the paraffin stove beside him.

The doctor awoke with a start. There was a knocking at the door. While he searched for his false teeth and fitted them into his mouth the knocking began again.

"I'm coming," he said loudly.

It took him some time to reach the door; the room was now completely dark, and because he had slept very deeply the furniture seemed to be in unfamiliar places.

The laird's factor, Jefferson, stood outside the door with his wife, and Magnus looked at them both with a blank unfocused stare.

"Ah," said the factor, "we thought perhaps you'd forgotten—"

"You asked us to drinks, now, remember?" Mrs. Jefferson said gaily.

"Ah, yes," he said, "I remember." He led the way through

the cottage door. "I apologize for the disorder in here, Mrs. Jefferson. If you will be so kind as to help me light a few candles around the place, we can all sit down and be comfortable."

It was biting cold and the candles flickered in every draft that came through the gaps in the doorframe. The factor sat totally silent on the edge of a chair and gazed at the floor in front of him, as though the entire state of the room and every piece of furniture in it alarmed and disgusted him. Mrs. Jefferson also leaned forward in her chair and shouted at the doctor, who, because of his age, she imagined to be deaf. Magnus began to mix a little whisky with the sherry he was drinking, and when he could bear Mrs. Jefferson's conversation no longer, he removed his false teeth again and wrapped them in a dirty handkerchief which he put into his pocket.

When the Jeffersons had left, he stumbled back in the flickering light toward his rocking chair, where he sat for a time biting his nails. Presently he began to drink again, and briefly, before he was totally drunk, Magnus imagined that Meriel Finlay was somewhere in the cottage and that in a little while she would come into the room with a paraffin lamp and lead him upstairs to bed.

In spite of his drunkenness, for several hours that night he was unable to sleep. He lay on his bed, fully dressed, and with his eyes wide open like a corpse. His head was spinning and his throat was dry. From time to time certain snatches of the past day came back to him; between them the gaps in his memory were total. These gaps were like stones, thrown high into the air, which never hit the solid ground.

19

In small places news travels so fast that at times it seems to be carried less by word of mouth than by the wind.

By noon, the laird's housekeeper had heard in full the story of the village priest and Meriel Finlay. This story she kept to herself, however, for it did not concern her. She had the lunch to prepare and a pie to get ready for the evening meal. But occasionally she would stand by the window, with her work in her hands, a piece of dough she was kneading or a vegetable half-peeled, and she would gaze with a puzzled frown into the kitchen yard.

When Meriel came into the room, she did not look up. She was making a steak and kidney pie. Her hands and the front of her apron were covered with flour.

"What's that?" Meriel asked. She watched Mrs. Mackinnon roll out the pastry on a marble slab. "I hope it's steak and kidney pie—I have a passion for it."

The housekeeper pursed her lips.

"It is," she said after a while.

Meriel sat down on a corner of the table. Without looking at her, Mrs. Mackinnon could sense a restless vitality in her. She seemed ready to burst out laughing or to spring up without warning and walk about the room.

"How old were you when you married Jock?" Meriel asked presently.

"Nineteen."

With one hand Mrs. Mackinnon took up the pie dish and with a knife she trimmed around the sides. Loose strips of pastry fell in neat crescents onto the table.

"Were you really nineteen? Imagine—how extraordinary." Suddenly Meriel began to laugh, as if there were something amusing in this, or a sly and unexpected joke had just then come into her head.

"Uh, huh, nineteen," said Mrs. Mackinnon.

The pastry, when glazed with an egg, would be a fine honey color, and the meat inside it a rich dense brown. She sighed and put down the dish.

"Well, then," she said. "What's on your mind?"

Meriel flushed vividly. She slid off the table and went to lean against the windowsill.

"Well, when you were in love—" she began. But here the words sounded trite to her and she did not go on.

"In love? Well, who could you be in love with?" Mrs. Mackinnon said crossly. "You talk as though it were some kind of disease. . . . I've no time for such nonsense," she added under her breath.

But Meriel was not paying attention. She started to speak several times and then suddenly stopped.

"What would you do—" she began.

And then a minute later she said, "And if someone asked you to go away with him—someone you loved—not to marry perhaps but just to leave with him, would you go?"

Mrs. Mackinnon straightened up from her work. She arranged the knife, the pastry brush, and the mixing bowl in a straight line in front of her. And then she looked across the table at Meriel. Her face was bright with anger.

"I have heard rumors today," she said steadily, "that I wouldn't credit. I would have none of them. Such a girl, I said, brought up a good Catholic, and coming from the best of families, would not be doing such things. Not with a Catholic priest."

Meriel did not even flinch. She gave the housekeeper a smile that was vague and sweet.

"But we love each other," she said simply.

Mrs. Mackinnon was now so angry that she picked up the mixing bowl in both hands and slammed it down on the table.

"That's no way to be talking," she cried, "about a priest of the Catholic church. There is love, yes, but that's not love, that's sinning. Sinning against your own family and sinning against the church. I wish," she added, "that the Lord might hear you."

Meriel remained unmoved. Indeed, for the time being, she seemed to enclose herself in some place where Mrs. Mackinnon and the present reality did not exist. There was a look of obstinate happiness in her face which made the housekeeper fling up her hands in despair.

"I see it's of no use talking to you," she said. "I've just been wasting my time and breath. I'm late with the lunch too. If you don't mind now, I'll get on with it."

Her anger was spent. She felt drained of the necessary energy to go on with the day ahead of her. She picked up the dirty dishes listlessly and took them to the sink. While she was washing them she looked out of the window again. The first trees around the house were changing color. A few dead leaves, stirred up by the wind, scattered outward across the yard.

"God help us," she said to no one in particular.

When she turned around, the room was empty. Meriel had gone. She sat down in a chair and closed her eyes.

"The truth is," she said later to her husband, "the truth is, I knew what was going on from a long way back." And after a while she came to believe it, although the truth was entirely different. The truth was that she had been blind and foolish. When all the events of the past few weeks were added together, Mrs. Mackinnon could clearly see what had been going on—so clearly that it now astonished her.

When Nealie the maid came into the room she got up from the chair.

"I'm going out," she said.

Nealie seemed startled.

"Everything's ready," she went on quickly. "The vegetables in the slow oven and the chops in the one above. Take care with the gravy dish," she added as an afterthought. "I've just noticed there's a crack in it."

"When'll you be back?" Nealie asked.

"When I'm ready," she answered sharply. "Good and ready."

She took her coat from the back hall peg and walked out into the fresh air. For some time she walked without taking her eyes from the road. She couldn't think what to do now. A while ago there had been nothing on her mind but the cooking, and now this trouble rose up in front of her like a mountain, and beyond it, on the other side, she could make out nothing at all. What if they eloped, the two of them? What if the child were already pregnant? What then? And the priest? What of the priest? She shook her head. To these questions and to others which she later asked herself she did not have the answers.

There was one man, however, in whom she had abiding faith, and this was her husband Jock. And here it is necessary, briefly, to describe him.

For, in the same way that a single pebble, lightly thrown, may start an avalanche, so it was Jock Mackinnon's advice which set in train the tragedy that followed.

Jock Alistair Mackinnon was a man of great physical

strength. He was tall, his shoulders were broad, and his hair was bright red and tightly curled. Throughout the peninsula he was admired for his sound judgment and for his honesty. And if there was a certain blindness in these qualities it was noticed by almost no one, and least of all by his wife.

Now Mrs. Mackinnon, by the time she reached home, had decided on a certain course. She would listen to her husband's advice, and together they would treat the matter in its proper light—as a sorry rumor without implications.

At once, however, the head stalker took a different attitude. He listened attentively while she spoke, and afterward he was silent for a minute. When he spoke again, his wife felt a chill pass through her like a cold draft that had suddenly come in through an open door.

The gossip must be stopped. Things would get worse, he assured her, far worse, unless the laird's son put an end to them. They would have to be nipped in the bud—he repeated this phrase too in a measured way, as though the whole core of the matter lay there. Having spoken at length, the head stalker went on with his meal and dismissed these questions entirely from his mind.

Some time later Mrs. Mackinnon went back to the big house to cook the evening meal. The day had lightened at last. A weak sunlight filtered through the trees along the road and their shadows fell in thin strips across the ground. And in the fields to either side of her, the autumn grass shook gently in the wind. Mrs. Mackinnon took no comfort whatsoever from such things. She sensed a treachery in the weather, a sweet and dangerous warmth. And beyond that mild September evening she could not forget the long winter that stretched ahead.

She waited until the dinner was served and eaten. And then about nine o'clock she sent Nealie upstairs to turn down the beds, and went herself through the baize door and into the outer hall.

Outside the study door she waited for a moment. No sound came from the room. She patted her hair and straightened out the folds of her apron. Then she knocked on the door and went in.

Charles Finlay was alone. Meriel was not about, and the old man had been taken back to his room immediately after dinner. Mrs. Mackinnon closed the door behind her and stood waiting with her hands folded until her employer looked up.

"What can I do for you?" Finlay asked her.

In a chair by the fire, he was reading from a sheaf of loose papers. These papers concerned the accounts of the syndicate shoot, and he disliked any interruption while he was reading them.

"It's about Miss Meriel," the housekeeper said. But having started she could not go on. The words sounded loose in her throat. The room too, which had been familiar to her all her life, now seemed oddly arranged. Certain pieces of furniture looked out of place and others which she normally took for granted now stuck out strangely.

"Well—go on."

Charles Finlay looked briefly into his housekeeper's face. And he saw there an expression of fear which startled him. He got up from his chair by the fire and went toward his desk. "Well, what is it?" he said impatiently. He had placed himself behind his desk so that the late evening setting sun shone full into his housekeeper's face while he himself stood to one side, in the shadows.

"It's this way . . . it's like this, sir." Mrs. Mackinnon now stared at the floor and twisted the corner of her apron about in one hand. "It seems," she went on, "that Miss Meriel is having a love affair with the priest."

To her astonishment he bent forward for a minute and scribbled something on a sheet of paper beside him on the desk. He put the pen back in the inkstand and shut the lid with a snap.

"What rubbish is this?" he asked her finally. "What nonsense are you repeating?"

"I don't think it's nonsense, sir," she said bravely. "I think it's the truth, so help me. She was seen last night in the woods with Father James."

"By whom?"

"By Morag, the housekeeper."

Finlay gave a loud snort of laughter.

"Hah, then you see—and if that is the only source of your information—"

Mrs. Mackinnon straightened her shoulders and fixed her employer with a sad, firm look.

"There are others," she said, "other sources besides. Nealie, for instance. One night when Morag was away, Miss Meriel's bed was not slept in. She was out all night."

"And then?"

"And then," she said finally with a sigh, "I have heard the truth, sir; I have heard it from Miss Meriel herself."

Charles Finlay came suddenly around the corner of the desk. He stumbled on a piece of carpet and recovered his balance. In spite of this he moved so fast that she had no time to get out of his way. He took her by the shoulders and began to shake her. "Shut up," he whispered. "Shut up, shut up, shut up."

His face caught a sudden angle of sunlight. The skin was tightly stretched across the bones, and it had the greenish hue of soft, wet clay. A fresh gust of wind began to rattle at the windowpanes, and on the same wind a thin cold draft came into the room from beneath the mahogany door.

20

Father James had spent a day of acute depression, and in the course of the late afternoon he had reached a sudden crisis. That afternoon, while he was drinking tea with one of his parishioners, the priest had done something unaccountable. In the middle of a sentence he had got up from his chair, murmured some brief excuse, and walked out of the house. For suddenly, while sitting alone with this old lady, he had longed to confide in her, to confess everything; and even to imagine in her face an expression of sympathy and understanding. He had left in such a hurry that his coat, and a book she had lent him, were still in the old lady's sitting room.

After his evening meal the priest sat alone in his study. The depression had left him finally and in its place he felt a queer lightheadedness. He looked at the contents of the room around him in a mild, disinterested way, as though seeing these things for the first time and from a distance.

On his desk and among the folds of his wallet were the details of his transfer to another diocese. In less than two weeks' time, he was leaving Kintillo for a large industrial parish in the north of England. It was an area he had never been to and had scarcely even glanced at on a map. And in his present mood these facts were about as vital to him as a hill of beans. They were merely words to him, and they were words without a single image to support them. Something else disturbed him: a deep and irrational longing which the priest no longer resisted. He intended that night, before renouncing her entirely, to see Meriel Finlay again.

He knew exactly how it would be. He knew the house, and also where Meriel slept, for he had seen her once walking along the landing to her room. But to the details of his plan, his walk down the drive at night, and his methods of breaking in, Father James paid almost no attention. He saw instead the inside of the house and the darkened hallway, its upper landings lit by the thin beams of a waning moon. Keeping to the deepest shadows, he would walk noiselessly up the wide staircase and along the moonlit landing to her room. Opening the door slowly and very gradually, he would slip at last inside her room. And here his fantasies sharpened and became more explicit. He could see, in spite of the semidarkness, the position of the furniture in the room, the varying shades of the night; the same moon from a gap between the curtains, thrown in a strip of light across the floor. Finally, he saw Meriel asleep. On her face there would be a look of warmth and of animal comfort, so totally oblivious that if he leaned across the pillow to kiss her, she would neither stir nor feel his presence.

He sat in the twilight and waited for the darkness. Sitting by the window, it seemed necessary to watch for each separate fleck of the night to appear. And still he could see the long line of the bay, and each point and bay beyond, going south to Kyle. And when he looked around the study, although color had been drawn from the room and the shadows had deepened and merged together, he could still see well enough to pick out each crack in the walls and each mark of damp on the ceiling.

His back ached from sitting in the same position; the whole of his body felt numb, as though the blood were no longer circulating and had centered at last in a dense mass around his heart.

Morag had gone to bed some time ago. Out of boredom he had counted every step of the stairs as she went up to bed. There were fourteen of them, and on each tread her weight had given out a different creaking note. Later he listened to the sound of her movements in the passage upstairs. They seemed erratic, one footfall heavier than another, and each of her journeys to and from the bathroom was accompanied by a low sibilant muttering.

Slowly the rectory settled into a torpid silence. One noise after another, the vibration of the upstairs cistern, the water circulating in the pipes, had gradually faded. And now after a day of tension the priest felt drowsy and relaxed. In spite of his cramped position in the upright chair, his eyelids closed and his head fell sideways against the windowsill. While he slept he began to dream.

In the last of these dreams before waking, he was lying in his bed at home, and through the open window of his room the branches of a great hibiscus were growing in thick profusion. The leaves of the tree were a sickly green and its flowers pressed in big scarlet clusters around the window frames. The heat in the room was damp and oppressive and the silence total.

When he awoke it was daylight. At first he looked around him in disbelief. In the wake of this vivid and meaningless dream the room seemed quite without substance. The clothes he was wearing also seemed strange—a thick sweater and dark gray trousers. He could no longer remember changing into them, nor could he remember for some minutes why he was sitting there.

Suddenly and with a sense of shock he put a hand into one pocket. He felt there the edges of a letter. It was the letter he had written to Meriel Finlay. And then he remembered the evening before, and the wild notion he had had to slip this letter under her pillow while she slept. But the morning had come and he had done nothing. With every minute that passed, the room was becoming lighter. Already the shadows had faded and the colors around him were stronger and more distinct. For a moment Father James gave in to an extraordinary panic. His face flushed and his hands began to tremble: he had left things too late to set out now in the daylight, for he was certain to be seen going into the house. And yet it was unthinkable to leave without seeing her. He felt this indecision so acutely that, without realizing what he was doing, he began to walk rapidly up and down the room—now deciding he would go immediately, now convinced that he could not do it.

Finally he took the letter and went toward the fireplace. He took a box of matches from the mantelpiece and firmly struck a light. He was about to hold this light to a corner of the letter when he looked up quickly as though something had disturbed him. He blew out the match and put the letter back into his pocket. With peculiar vividness he had seen Meriel. Not in a way in which he had ever known her, but in some unaccountable danger. She was running toward him across the open fields, and in her face he could briefly see a look of rootless terror.

He sat down and covered his face with his hands.

"That's nonsense," he said aloud. "That's all nonsense."

Nevertheless, he now wanted to see her more than ever. He wanted to assure himself that Meriel still lay as he had imagined her, in a deep untroubled sleep. He was afraid for her in some vague way he could not describe. And now, sitting in the silent room, it seemed to the priest that his fears were caused not by his own heightened nervousness but by certain forces outside himself, by some insidious warning in the atmosphere which he could not explain. At the same time a strange apathy came over him, so that he went on sitting, without moving, in the chair.

When he looked up at last and went to the window, the daylight had finally come. The peaks of the Cuillins were clear across the water. To the north of them, to the east and to the south, other mountains, colorless in the early sun, rose steeply from the sea.

I should go now, he thought. I should really go.

But he stayed a little longer looking out of the window.

It was half past four in the morning when Meriel awoke. She awoke quite suddenly, as though someone had called her name. And afterward she lay without moving in the bed, for it seemed to her that the silence was incomplete and that presently this voice, on the same high note, would call out to her again. But the sound was not repeated. There was nothing outside her window but the sound of the first birds among the trees around the house. First, one close by among the branches of a great magnolia, and then others farther away among the fringes of the woods. While she listened to them she smiled. It seemed to her that in the wake of each song a tree would bloom and take shape again after the night.

Presently, she put on her slippers and dressing gown and went to the window. The sky was a light clear gray, and below it the line of Raasay was flat against the sea. On such mornings the light would draw downward from the peaks across the coast of Skye; the sea from gray would turn to a frail pure blue and the birds would spread their full wingspan when the sun had risen and begin their hunt for food. But there were other mornings, cold and dense, when the light lifted slowly like a mist, from the ground upward. Certain shapes appeared gradually and in a certain order: the line of trees along the wall of the park, the creeks and hollows of the bay, and then finally the islands in the Inner Sound. On those mornings the sea was calm and sullen, confined to a space without horizons. But now the dawn was cloudless, and in less than an hour the sun would light up the sound and the Inner Hebrides beyond it.

Her window faced south: the rectory was out of sight, on the side of the hill. And yet her whole attention was drawn toward it as though she were there in the room watching the priest while he slept. When she thought of him she was filled with an extraordinary happiness. This happiness made her restless, so that it was no longer possible to stay dreaming by the window or to go back again to her bed. Without having the slightest idea where she would go, she began to dress hurriedly, and a few minutes later with her shoes in one hand she went down the stairs into the dark hall. By the door she slipped on her shoes and a coat from the peg and went out.

The hinges of the front door creaked when she shut it behind her, and she stood for a moment listening on the steps outside. The gun dogs lived in the stables. At the faintest sound they would bark and fling themselves at the tack room door. Her father, too, slept lightly. He would sometimes wake up when she went out in the early morning and she would see his face at the bedroom window as she was going across the park.

She kept to the grass verges along the edge of the house and walked on the drive where the gravel was thin and worn into ruts. From time to time she looked back at her father's window which faced west over the sound and to the north across the side woods and the open valley. Because of the early hour and the emptiness of the park around her she felt a certain guilty pleasure, as if she were doing something expressly forbidden.

In the darkness of the woods a pheasant rose from the bushes close to the path, and its disconnected cry seemed to scatter out across the whole of the valley. The noise startled her, and she walked on more cautiously until she came to the bridge across the river. From the rickety wooden bridge the path ran through the trees into the flat marsh fields of the valley bottom.

Meriel took the road to loch Doonican. From the heights of the small peat loch she would see the coast of Skye and the line of the mainland going south to Kyle. She would sit by the empty shooting lodge along the shore and raise her face to the first warmth of the sun when it came up across the rim of Torridon. She walked so lightly on the ground that she seemed to float above it, and each step carried her forward with a strange weightlessness.

When she was still a child the summer had seemed like this; the mornings gray, the sunsets violent and queerly colored, and the days themselves cloudless and without wind. In those summers they had spent all day, she and Anne, on the empty beaches. They would take picnics down to the edge of the shore and fool around there until it was warm enough to bathe. And with the same uncomplicated joy she felt now, Meriel would run out across the sand too fast to stop herself from wading clear into the sea. The fierce cold of the water would shock her, and at the same time she would burst out laughing as the spray shot up around her in the sun. But now she despised this former happiness and even thought of it with pity. For she had been easily satisfied. In the course of a single warm day she had forgotten the weeks of rain that had preceded it.

Now her emotions were of another caliber. They were deeper and more intense. They had roots to them, or a single solid base: her mind and heart were totally concerned with the priest, and her feelings were directed toward him in the same natural way that a flower in the shadows of a room would turn toward the light.

The fenced-in fields of the valley were now below her, and the brown wastes of the moors came down to the edges of the

road. The moors were pitted with bogs and deep hollows
which were as neat and as round as wells. From these hollows
the marsh birds rose up into the morning sun. Meriel began
to sing to herself aloud; although the song was sad, she sang it
gaily and in a high lilting voice:

> Early one morning, just as the sun was rising
> I saw a maiden singing in the valley below
> Oh don't deceive me
> Oh never leave me
> How could you use u—u—use a poor maiden so.

There was only one verse to it, a verse of five lines, and she
sang it without thinking over and over again. There were no
trees around the peat loch Doonican, nothing to retain the
sound. Her voice seemed to stop a few feet from her, and the
silence of the empty moors remained unbroken.

Charles Finlay had heard his daughter go out, for he had
been awake throughout the long, pale night. He heard the
latch of her bedroom door open and gently close again. He
had heard the stair treads creak and the hinges of the great
front door hiss and swing shut behind her. He listened to
these things without surprise, for he told himself that
everything was now clear to him—not only what had
previously taken place, but the exact order of the events that
would follow. He knew Meriel was walking up the road
toward the rectory, and that in a few minutes the priest
would appear in the doorway and let her into the house. At
the thought of the priest, an odd smile crossed his face, and in
the dimness of the room this smile resembled the fixed grin
on the face of a stiffened corpse.

Presently he got up and started to dress. He dressed
without hurrying and in his normal methodical fashion.
Since the early morning was certain to be damp and cold,

Finlay took from his cupboard a pair of plus fours and a thick tweed jacket. There was nothing in his mind at all. It was a total blank fixed only on the task in hand, as though one set of actions, however trivial, were now as important as another. When he was dressed, he took his stiletto from a table, and into the breast pocket of his jacket he tucked a loosely folded handkerchief. Finally he stood for a minute looking out of the window. Like someone in a dream, he saw nothing. His vision was turned inward and his face was calm and even cold.

Before he left, his eyes wandered slowly around the room as though there were something he had forgotten which he would shortly remember. In his chest of drawers there was a box of shotgun shells. He took two of these from the box and slipped them into his left-hand pocket. From a corner of the room, by the cupboard, he took his shotgun and held it lightly in the crook of his arm. After a moment's thought, however, he opened the chambers and lifted it to the light. Both barrels were clean and well oiled. Finlay sighed and rearranged the gun on his arm.

Once again he looked around the room before going out and shutting the door quietly behind him.

Outside, the sun had fully risen. The dew was heavy on the ground, and the whole park glistened in the fresh morning light. But Finlay noticed nothing, for his reactions were hardened and blunted by shock. In this state of shock, which had been with him throughout the night, he again told himself that he understood everything and that what he had to do was both right and inevitable. He carried his gun easily and naturally, and his eyes were fixed on the drive in front of him as he walked along.

A keen wind was coming in from the west and the wash of a storm at sea rolled in across the wide mouth of the bay. The sound of the sea was as natural to him as the sound of his own breathing and he neither looked up nor lessened his speed against the force of the rising wind. Something else, scarcely audible, attracted him—the sound of footsteps coming down the rectory hill.

When he looked up and saw the priest, he noticed first the clothes he was wearing, a thick Arran sweater and a pair of gray corduroy trousers. His hair was ruffled by the wind and shone brightly in the early sun. In his right hand he was holding a white envelope, and this too caught the light. Finlay took in these details in the same way that a man might notice the moss or the patterns in the brickwork of a well down which he was falling.

In the time it took for the priest to look up at him, Charles Finlay had loaded the gun and raised it to his shoulder. At a distance of thirty yards he aimed for the center of the priest's forehead and fired. Father James fell forward into the road without a sound. A few pebbles scattered loose around his body and ran free for a little way among the ruts of the road.

Finlay ejected the shells from the gun and stood for an instant motionless in the road. He neither looked up at the point where the priest had fallen, nor did he think of him. Something perplexed him. In the few seconds before firing, a sound had disturbed him. In the lull of the wind he had heard a voice singing across the valley fields. But now, though he listened, the singing had stopped.